To Isabel

N
E
S
DEORSK OCEAN
KATANOS
TELEOS
ANALIKA
MEGON
SOUTH EMPHIDIAN RANGE
OLAC
PRINCIPALITIES OF THE CRUSADE
GATINA
CRESCENTIUM
THE AZURE COAST
THE GREY ROCK
THANAGOST PEAKS
GULF OF MARAZI'D
KIRI UMOOR
the lands of LEGEND
MUNGODA RIVER
THE UNCHARTED CONTINENT OF MUNGODA
PARU
COSH GOYOPE SWAMP

RIVER FELDA
ASMULIA
EASTERN STEPPES
THE SLEETMARSH
IBRAHIM
CALIPHATE of ZHENIR
ASUN
HAKBAD
DHULAN
DEMKHOR
HARGARN MTNS
CITADEL OF THE SHADOWLORDS
GONHALA PLAIN
SWAMPS of THE JINN
KAIKUHURAN DESERT
EMIRATE of MARAZID
TA'AQAN
FORTRESS of ALAFLAK
UT
KISE
RIVER ISIS
AMSA'IM
AQA'ALA
SULTANATE of OPALAR
TO BATUBATAN, ZINJ AND KHITAI
THE DEEPS OF RASAKNA

Contents

The Magi

Now as at all times I can see in the mind's eye,
In their stiff, painted clothes, the pale unsatisfied ones
Appear and disappear in the blue depth of the sky
With all their ancient faces like rain-beaten stones,
And all their helms of silver hovering side by side,
And all their eyes still fixed, hoping to find once more,
Being by Calvary's turbulence unsatisfied,
The uncontrollable mystery on the bestial floor.

W. B. Yeats

The Story So Far

Altor, a young warrior-monk, has been entrusted with the jewelled pommel stone of the Sword of Life. This magical weapon is said to be the only thing that can overcome the Five Magi – ancient wizards who, banished from the earth, have transformed themselves into baleful comets in the night sky.

After falling in with Caelestis, a dashing rogue who lives by his wits, Altor travelled to the Kingdom of Wyrd in search of the Sword of Life's hilt. There the two heroes learned from a prophecy that they would find the last part, the blade itself, in 'a city of spires and domes beside an azure bay'.

And so they have travelled south to Crescentium, the Crusaders' foothold in the Holy Land, to find the fragment that will finally allow them to reconstruct the fabled Sword of Life.

Prologue

The heat of the day had long since fled from the desert, and under a sky of a million stars a man stood on the white sands beside a corpse.

In the man's hand was a long knife, gently curved, whose blade shone dark and wet in the cold moonlight. Stooping, he dipped the knife in the corpse's gaping chest and used its blood to draw a circle around where it lay.

The task done, he raised his eyes to the heavens and spoke seventeen syllables in a guttural tongue.

A wind rose, pulling ripples of fine sand across the moon-bleached dunes.

The man directed the knife in turn to each point of the compass, his movements as graceful and precise as those of a dancer or a beast of prey. And as he turned he seemed to sing a spell under his breath in the same exotic language.

At his feet, the corpse's eyelids rolled open and it stared in blind horror at the stars.

The spell ended. The man thrust the knife towards the sky, uttering as he did a mighty shout.

A star fell. In the moment of its falling, the man spoke to the corpse: 'All of an instant is our entering and leaving of this world. I have sent you into the great darkness. Tell me now what you behold there. Give answers that will throw light on the riddles of days yet to come.'

A groan rose from the corpse's pallid lips – deep and long and tortured, escaping from a well of inexpressible grief – and gradually this terrible sound took the form of words.

'Three questions will I answer,' boomed

the corpse. 'Then let me escape into the bosom of Death.'

'Agreed. Tell me first: what news of my foes? You know the two of which I speak.'

'One has died already, the other soon will die.'

In the moonlight, the man's eyes shone like alabaster. 'What? Am I to be cheated of my revenge, then?'

'No,' groaned the corpse. 'You will have vengeance, but only for a time, and in the sight of countless eyes you will renounce it.'

'Nonsense. You speak in riddles.'

'Why should I not? You have put out my sight for ever, and yet you ask me to look into your future. Ask your last question and let my soul depart.'

The man shook his head. Then, remembering that the corpse's eyes could no longer see the things of this world, he gave a soft chuckle. Unhooking a silver bottle from his belt, he took out its stopper and crouched to hold it above the dead lips.

'Your soul? That stained revenant? Cough it out!'

A dark swirl, like a tattered scrap of night, escaped from the corpse's mouth and was sucked into the bottle.

The man smiled and put back the stopper. 'For a while I think I'll keep you, like a fly, in this bottle. I must have answers to these riddles before I pose my third question. Then you'll have the peace you crave – and I'll have my revenge on Altor of Ellesland and that trickster Caelestis.'

ONE

THE HOLY LAND

The city was a maze of streets, market squares, bazaars and alleyways that rose in tiers between the buildings of hard-baked clay, stone and patterned brickwork. Under the shadowed colonnade of a hostel, merchants and pilgrims sat listless in the day's fierce heat.

The two friends emerged from the fetid confines of yet another winding alley to find themselves gazing out over the seafront.

'Back where we started!' cried Caelestis with feeling. He threw his hat to the ground and slumped down on a heap of sacks.

Altor wiped the sweat from his brow and

looked around. It was indeed the same stretch of quay where they had disembarked only that morning. White sails slid majestically across a cobalt harbour, enclosed by fortified walls like the flanks of a great armoured dragon. Altor turned his head. Above rose the minarets and jewelled domes, shimmering in the dusty haze of late afternoon sunlight like etchings on a gold plate.

It was here, Altor felt sure, that they would find the lost blade of the Sword of Life.

Caelestis seemed to read his mind. 'It's not here,' he growled. 'Do you know how many cities in the world lie "beside an azure bay"? It's one of those others, not Crescentium.'

Altor knew better than to argue with his friend who, when tired and out of sorts, could be stubborn indeed. 'We've only been looking for a few hours,' he pointed out. 'It's too much to hope that the blade would just be lying in the street for us to stumble over.'

Caelestis retrieved his hat, scowling at the dust and sweat that had accumulated on it during their long afternoon's slog through the twisting streets. As he did so, his gaze fell on the magic ring he wore. Briefly he considered rubbing the jewel, calling out the occupant that dwelt in its smoky depths . . .

'Let's ask the Faltyn, then,' said Altor, seeing Caelestis eye the ring thoughtfully.

Caelestis jumped to his feet in irritation. 'What? Then we'd have to give it the last of our money and we'd have nothing left to pay for passage on a ship out of here.'

Altor counted out the contents of his money pouch. Forty silver florins. 'Not enough to get us back to Ferromaine,' he said. 'We'd better choose our next port of call carefully.'

Caelestis nodded, a little better-tempered now he'd had the chance to let off steam. 'We'll discuss it tonight over a meal and a glass of Opalar wine.'

As the sun sank below the harbour wall, the sound of church bells drifted over the rooftops, mixed with the poignant song of

Ta'ashim priests as they called the faithful to prayer.

'We'll need to find a place to spend the night, certainly,' said Altor. 'I have somewhere in mind, but I'm not sure if they serve wine. The monastery of the Knights Capellars, at the Temple of the Roc.'

Caelestis reeled back in exaggerated shock. 'A monastery? I need a bath, a hot meal, soft sheets . . . Not a bowl of gruel followed by an uncomfortable night on a wooden board!'

'At least it would be free,' said Altor, slipping the coins back into his money pouch.

Caelestis stared at him in fury. 'In the last three months we've slogged through snowdrifts in the Drakken foothills, crossed the Gouge, slept in any number of cheap lice-infested inns between the Rathurbosk Bridge and the Ferromaine League, then spent a month cramped inside a ship that stank of sweat and stagnant bilge-water. We've suffered rainstorms, icy winds, baking heat, thirst, discomfort. And now you expect me to spend the night in a monastery? Not a bit of it! I've put up with quite enough. For this one night I intend to sleep in luxury.'

Altor planted his hands on his hips. 'And how will you afford that?'

Caelestis smiled a self-assured smile. 'You take yourself off to the Knights Capellars. Don't worry about me – I have my resources. Tomorrow morning we'll meet outside the Temple of the Roc – and don't blame me if your back's stiff from sleeping on the floor of a monk's cell.'

So saying, he spun on his heel and strode off up the street they'd just come down.

At the top, Caelestis paused to take stock. A variety of smells assailed his nostrils, not all masked by the exotic spices and incense wafting from the traders' stalls. The effect was a curious contradiction that in many ways seemed symbolic of the city of Crescentium – squalid and splendid by turns, a place where grand palaces and temples soared above streets crammed with the hovels of beggars.

Caelestis was determined to enjoy the best the city had to offer. But how to achieve that without cost? Only a few months earlier he would have solved the problem simply by stealing what he needed, using his knife to slit the purse of some passing priest or merchant in gold-trimmed finery. That seemed unworthy of his noble quest, however, and he knew that Altor would disapprove. Also, he knew the penalties in Crescentium for even petty thievery.

'Jablo the Knife!' he said aloud, snapping his fingers as the name occurred to him.

Jablo had once stolen trinkets alongside Caelestis when they were children on the streets of Tamor. The last Caelestis had heard of him, he'd been involved in the jewellery trade here in Crescentium. Surely he would not object to a visit from an old friend.

Obtaining directions from a camel drover, Caelestis set out for the jewellers' market. At this hour the streets were full of people making their way to evening prayers in one of the city's countless churches and mosques, and it took him some time to struggle through them.

By the time he reached the market, red sunset laid a tangle of purple shadows under the branches of dusty cedar trees. The shutters were closed over the jewellers' shop windows. As dusk settled, the clangour of church bells died to a few distant chimes. The last notes of the call to prayer echoed over the rooftops and then faded with the sun.

Nearby a young lad scampered to and fro, trying to dislodge the shutter across one of the windows. Caelestis smiled indulgently, reminded of his own childhood. After a moment he cleared his throat.

The boy jumped into the air, ran off a few paces, then looked back warily.

'Tell me, lad, do you know where Jablo the Knife lives?'

The boy thought for a moment, then grinned. 'Cost you.'

Caelestis frowned. As an idea came to him,

he glanced furtively over his shoulder, leaned closer to the boy and put his finger to his lips. 'This is very *hush-hush*, lad. I'm on a secret mission for the Ferromaine League. It's vital I find Jablo at once.'

The boy looked dubious. 'Are you a *spy*, then?'

'You know Jablo. Surely an astute lad such as yourself must have realised there was something shady about him?'

'I always thought he was just a crook.'

Caelestis put on a wry smile. 'Ah, clever Jablo. The perfect cover for someone in our profession.' He nodded reflectively.

'What's your mission?' asked the boy, his eyes widening as he started to accept Caelestis' yarn.

'That I cannot say. Too many others have died already. Best if you never speak of it to a living soul.'

'Will I have to be sworn to secrecy?'

'Hmm. Not just that, but I think I must instate you as an emergency operative of the Ferromaine League. Do you agree to uphold the principles of Justice, Truth and Free Enterprise?'

The boy, by now thoroughly confused as well as excited, nodded quickly. 'Jablo awaits you in that building across the square. The rooms on the first landing.'

Caelestis put his hand on the boy's shoulder. 'Excellent. Now slip quietly home and be ready to receive further orders.'

As the boy darted off, Caelestis turned to size up the building he had pointed out. It was a tall tenement of pale-coloured bricks with a forecourt of cracked ceramic tiles.

The faithful were now ensconced in their temples, the faithless in their taverns. With the crowds thinned out and the dry, stifling heat of the day giving way to the cool of evening, Caelestis felt more relaxed. Jauntily he loped across the square and up the steps to the first landing, where he rapped on the door.

There was a long pause. An old Ta'ashim man opened the door a crack and looked

Caelestis up and down in the twilight filtering through the decorative casement over the stairwell.

'You want Jablo?' said the old man, his voice thickly accented.

Caelestis nodded.

'Next floor.'

The door was shut in his face. Caelestis sighed and climbed another flight of stairs, less briskly this time. Another door faced him. He knocked and waited, but there was no answer.

Caelestis had no intention of waiting on the landing until Jablo returned home. He inserted his dagger in the lock and jiggled it around until he heard a click. He leaned on the door. It swung open, admitting him to an elegant apartment whose floor was strewn with thick velvet cushions. Silk drapes partitioned the room and hid its drab brick walls. By the window stood a stout cupboard with ivory panels set into its doors.

Caelestis was on the point of finding a

bottle of wine and settling down to wait, but there was a tiny nagging doubt at the back of his mind. Something was not right, but he couldn't immediately place it. He surveyed the room again, this time noting that the drapes were embroidered with pictures of voluptuous houris disporting themselves in the gardens of the Ta'ashim paradise. It was an unlikely decorative motif to find in the room of Jablo the Knife, whom Caelestis remembered as something of a prude.

Caelestis rubbed his jaw. Wasn't it possible the years in Crescentium had broadened Jablo's outlook? By way of confirmation he threw open the wardrobe. It was filled with brocade gowns, scented silk blouses, wispy skirts and jewelled copper breast-cups . . .

Caelestis had been duped. Obviously a woman lived here. Then it hit him. The 'old Ta'ashim man' in the room below – *that* had been Jablo!

'By all the hallows!' cried Caelestis. He raced from the room and went down the steps three at a time. Jablo, still in his disguise as a Ta'ashim elder, was just about to slip out into the dusk.

'One moment, "Grandad",' snarled Caelestis, seizing him by the shoulder and shoving him to the back of the stairwell.

Jablo winced. 'Caelestis! Not so rough, if you please.'

Caelestis pressed him even more tightly against the banister. 'Too busy to say hello to an old friend these days, eh, Jablo?'

'Of course I'd have welcomed you with open arms if not for the danger . . .'

'What danger?' scoffed Caelestis.

'I have to meet some accomplices to talk business. They wouldn't appreciate you sticking your nose in. Most likely they'd cut it off for you.'

'I don't care about your business. I just need a place to spend the night.'

'You can't stay here. I'll be coming back with the merchandise later.'

Caelestis nodded decisively. 'In that case I'll

tag along with you and my nose will take its chances.'

Jablo nodded sourly and led the way outside, only to set up a hue and cry: 'Help! My life is threatened! Help me!'

Some soldiers of the city militia sauntered over. Caelestis, realising trouble was afoot, looked around for an avenue of escape. Unfortunately three Knights Capellars had also heard the commotion and were striding up behind.

'What's all this?' one of the watchmen asked Jablo. 'Who's threatening your life, old man?'

'Have pity on a poor beggar, sir,' wheezed Jablo. He pointed at Caelestis. 'This person is the notorious Jablo the Knife, the most daring jewel-thief in all Crescentium.'

The watchmen fanned out, surrounding Caelestis. Not far off, the three Capellars watched silently. With the last pink scar of afterglow along the rooftops behind them, they looked like three Angels of Death waiting at the lip of the Inferno.

'Look for the mole on the villain's jawline,' urged Jablo as he slipped away. 'Even Jablo the Knife, a master of disguise, cannot hide that!'

A barrel-bellied watchman, whom Caelestis took to be the sergeant, raised his night-lamp and peered at him in the twilight. 'Yes, there's a mole, all right,' he grunted. 'Jablo the Knife, you're under arrest.'

'What?' shrieked Caelestis. 'You blundering fat oaf. That mole is my own. Have you ever heard any description of Jablo the Knife? He doesn't have a mole!'

'How would you know?' said the sergeant, in a tone of voice that Caelestis ought to have recognised as dangerous.

'I'm well acquainted with Jablo. We've known each other since childhood.' Caelestis blinked, wondering why he had said that.

'So, if you're not Jablo in person, you admit you're his accomplice? Either way, you're under arrest.'

If Caelestis had learned one thing in his

life, it was not to waste time arguing with city militia. He snatched the night-lamp and dashed it to the ground. The watchmen scattered in panic as burning oil spilled out around their feet.

Caelestis darted away, froze by instinct, and ducked as a sword-blade whispered through the air centimetres above his head. It was one of the Knights Capellars. Although himself a skilled swordsman, Caelestis was no match for warriors of their calibre. He pulled off his cloak, flung it in the Capellars' faces, and ran off across the square.

He ran until he was quite sure he had lost them. Leaning on a barrel by the side of the road to get his breath back, he counted the cost of his run-in with Jablo. He had lost the gold-threaded cloak he'd bought in Ferromaine, dropped his hat while running, and now the militia would probably post a warrant for Jablo's arrest using Caelestis' description.

And, worst of all, the Knights Capellars

were looking for him. How could he make his rendezvous with Altor now? If he showed himself at the Temple of the Roc they would kill him on sight.

TWO

The Sailor's Story

Altor's evening had been very different. At the Temple of the Roc he found a quadrangle teeming with warriors clad in chain mail despite the leaden heat. One of the Knights Capellars, seeing him enter the gates, came striding over. He made the sign of the cross look like a military salute.

Altor explained he was a warrior-monk of Ellesland and needed a place to stay the night.

'You're welcome here, brother,' said the knight. He shouted something and a Ta'ashim servant came scurrying. 'Go with this fellow. He will take you to the commandant.'

The servant conducted Altor into a high-roofed hall behind the quadrangle. It was like stepping into a cool bath as he passed out of the ruddy blaze of sunset, and the shadows deliciously enfolded him. Altor breathed a sigh of relief.

'Does hardship not agree with you, then?' snapped a stern voice. A grim-faced knight stepped forward and sized Altor up. 'If you seek to join the Capellars, young man, you must learn to tolerate the extremes of heat and cold – aye, and all other discomforts. We are prepared to die for Our Lord. Compared to that vow, the desire for luxury is merely frivolous.'

'In fact I do not wish to join,' said Altor, adding hastily when he saw the glare in the knight's eyes, 'I am already a novitiate of the Leandrine Order.'

'The Leandrines, eh?' The knight nodded, slightly mollified, though he still looked like a wolfhound with an evil temper. 'Not a bad lot of warriors, I suppose. You've just arrived in Outremer, I suppose?'

'Outremer?'

'The Holy Land. But we Capellars have sworn never to call it by that name till every Ta'ashim heathen has been driven into the Gulf of Marazid.' He spat on the floor. 'I am Tobias of Vantery, provincial commander of the Capellar Order here in Crescentium.'

'Altor of Osterlin.'

'Well, Altor of Osterlin, if you have come seeking hospitality you'll soon find we don't go in for soft indulgence at the Temple of the Roc. The Knights Capellars are the soldiers of God. Hard tack, hard beds and hard training are the principles we live by.'

'Of course.' Altor nodded politely. Secretly he recognized Tobias as a fanatic of the worst kind: one so immersed in his religion that he sees no goodness in others.

Tobias beckoned the servant as though swatting at a fly. 'Now you can sleep,' he said to Altor. 'Tomorrow at breakfast we will talk.'

The servant led the way into the further recesses of the hall. Altor made to follow, then hesitated and looked back to where Tobias stood outlined in the doorway against the pale evening sky.

'Sir Tobias, do you by any chance know anything of an artefact called the Sword of Life?'

Tobias did not even bother to turn around. After a long pause, he replied, 'Have I not said we will speak on the morrow? Patience is one of the seven virtues by which man comes closest to God's perfection, is it not?'

Altor doubted if it was but thought it wiser to say nothing. Shrugging, he bid Tobias good evening and followed the servant along a corridor. The man halted beside a threadbare tapestry, yanking it aside to reveal an alcove strewn with reed mats.

'It's good job Caelestis went off to find more comfortable accommodation,' said Altor aloud. 'He would never have tolerated a poky little hole like this.'

The Ta'ashim servant seemed to misunderstand Altor's words. Tugging at the young monk's sleeve, he led him to an opulent suite of apartments at the end of the corridor. High windows ran the length of the east wall, opening onto a veranda floored with delicate mosaic. Silk curtains patterned with sequins fluttered in the evening breeze.

'This is quite the lap of luxury!' declared Altor, looking around in amazement.

'The knights slept here before,' said the servant haltingly. 'Not now. New commandant, he says no. Blankets of horsehair for them.'

'Suffering is good for the soul, admittedly,' said Altor. 'But I think I've earned a spot of comfort for a change. Thank you, these chambers will suit me very well.'

'You want supper, master?' enquired the servant as he withdrew.

'Yes. And . . . oh, why not? Just the one glass of wine can't do any harm.'

As the servant scurried off to comply, Altor threw himself down on a satin-covered bed and yawned, sleepily content. Some monastery! Surely even Caelestis could not have found himself such an agreeable place to spend the night.

'Welcome to the Tower of the Throne of Purple. I am Alexius of Ferromaine, your host.'

Caelestis looked around the inn with open distaste. Its only claim to the title of 'tower' was that it was exceedingly narrow; the furnishings would not have been appropriate for any kind of throne that he would care to occupy, and as for Alexius – the way he leered at Caelestis in the yellow lamplight suggested a man of unwholesome personal habits.

In an alcove at the back, half a dozen sailors were squatting around a gaming board throwing dice. Caelestis' eyes strayed briefly to a shadowy corner of the room where a puffy-faced woman in violently coloured silks sat cradling a goblet of wine. She winked and showed a grey-toothed smile. Caelestis hastily turned his attention back to the host.

'Will you require food?' asked Alexius. 'A room? Anything that you need, you have only to ask.'

Caelestis surveyed a plateful of greasy buns on a table beside the sailors and shook his head. 'I'm hungry, but not *that* hungry. I'll take your best suite.'

Alexius licked his lips, his long jaw and rolling eyes making him look like a horse. 'I must warn you, sir, it is not cheap. For a night's lodging, whether you take breakfast or not, the fee is twenty florins.'

'Twenty florins? I could take ship to Ferromaine, reside in luxury there for a week, and still have change to spare!'

Alexius gave him a simpering smile. 'I very much doubt it, sir.'

'I'll give you one florin, two if the bed-sheets are clean.'

'The authorities are very strict, sir. I must stick to the agreed tariff, which is twenty florins.'

Caelestis stared around in amazement. 'But

this is absurd. Your hostel is a ramshackle slum. You cannot possibly expect me to pay that much. Oh, never mind, I'll take my custom elsewhere.'

Despite his gangling frame, Alexius skipped lightly enough to the door. 'Allow me to summon the watchmen, sir, and they can escort you safely to another establishment.' He stared Caelestis significantly in the eye.

Caelestis gritted his teeth. Somehow or other this wretch had tumbled to his secret. Naturally enough, in fact – why else would a stranger in fine clothes come in through Alexius' door, unless he was in trouble with the law? Inwardly Caelestis cursed himself for being careless, but he favoured Alexius with a smile. 'Let's make it twenty-five florins, and you can throw in a mug of ale for everyone here.'

The sailors heard this and raised a cheer. While Alexius went to fetch the ale, Caelestis strolled over to them. 'What is the game?' he asked.

'Hard-a'-port Hornpipe. You know the rules?'

Caelestis affected an expression of mild puzzlement. 'I'm sure I can learn, if you fellows will indulge me for the first few throws.'

The sailors laughed. 'Sure we will. Draw up a seat and join in.'

Caelestis' intention was to let the sailors win for a few throws before substituting the weighted dice that he kept up his sleeve. That way he hoped to sucker them into playing for high stakes. All the more worrying, then, when he found himself winning the first throw, and the second, and the third.

'Must be beginner's luck,' said one of the sailors. His lugubrious face was not entirely convincing.

'If this goes on we're ruined men,' said another, crying into his beer. Or was he crying? Caelestis peered at the man, a frown slowly clouding his face. The fellow's mouth was pressed to his cup and his shoulders were shaking, but whether from misery or mirth Caelestis could not tell.

Caelestis was not comfortable with games of chance. It was time to introduce the weighted dice. He shook his sleeve, dropped the dice into his palm, and went to switch them with the sailors' pair.

'More ale, gentlemen? Oh, I'm terribly sorry, sir.'

He looked round in annoyance. Alexius, coming up behind him with a tray of drinks, had splashed foam onto his velvet jerkin.

'Mind what you're doing! I—'

Caelestis jerked his gaze back to the gaming board. He had thought he saw a flicker of furtive movement out of the corner of his eye.

The sailors gazed back at him placidly. The man to his right pointed at two dice lying in front of Caelestis. 'Your roll, youngster,' he said with a broad smile.

Caelestis' heart sank. He knew that his winning streak had come to an end.

An hour later the sailors finally allowed

him to escape from the game. He had lost his waistcoat, a jewelled scarf-pin, the silver buckles off his boots – and, worst of all, the magic gold ring containing the Faltyn.

He had managed to salvage a few copper coins, in return for which Alexius led him to a dormitory at the back of the inn. The rows of cots contained an unsavoury assortment of drunken pilgrims, filthy street hawkers, crippled soldiers and pox-ridden wanderers. The smell of unwashed humanity was almost overpowering.

'Here is your bed. This pitcher contains fresh water,' said Alexius. His manner had changed since Caelestis lost his money. He pointed at a shuttered lamp. 'Do not extinguish that. Its fumes help to drive off biting insects.'

Caelestis watched him go, then sat down miserably on the bed. It comprised just a thin grubby sheet laid on a rickety wooden board. As Caelestis shifted his weight the bed made an agonized creaking sound, provoking a curse from someone dozing on the other side of the dormitory.

'Lovely,' said Caelestis, under his breath. 'I should have taken my chances at the monastery after all.'

'Do you know the port of Shahmir?' asked a voice out of the gloom.

Caelestis looked round. On the next bed perched a Ta'ashim sailor sucking a pipe.

'I was once on a ship bound for Shahmir,' the sailor went on. 'We carried our usual cargo of sandalwood, silk and ebony, and also we had a passenger, a learned sage from the land of Khitai. When he came aboard he brought with him a very large crate, which was placed in the hold.'

Caelestis had been on the point of telling the man to shut up, but now his curiosity got the better of him. 'What was in this crate?' he asked.

'Ah, I began to wonder just that. Day after day I brooded on it, till at last I could beat it no longer and I stole down into the hold. It was late at night and I was supposed to be on lookout. With a belaying pin I broke open the crate, and inside I found a statue of a horse made of ivory and ebony, as big as life.

'Even as I inspected this marvel the ship lurched, throwing me to one side, and I heard her timbers being split like brittle twigs. A cry went up, by which I knew we had encountered the Dendan, a monstrous fish that inhabits the Gulf. If only I had been at my post in the rigging I might have spotted it and given the signal to change course. But now, because I had succumbed to foolish curiosity, the ship and all of us aboard were surely doomed . . .'

The sailor puffed at his pipe, filling the space between them with reeking blue smoke.

The story reminded Caelestis of his own encounter with the sea serpent, Jormungand, in the Mistral Sea. 'And then?' he urged. 'How did you escape?'

'As you value what a poor wretch like me can tell you,' cried the sailor with sudden passion, 'be charitable. I have no belongings left in this world, save for these ragged clothes, my trusty pipe and a few grammes of hempweed.'

Caelestis tossed him a single copper penny. 'There is the last of my cash. It's no use to me, any more than half a drop of water will save a man dying of thirst. Now continue your tale.'

The sailor bit the coin before pocketing it. 'The ship was tossed to and fro across the waves by the monstrous fish, and I was flung into a corner of the hold. As I lay there, I beheld the Khitan sage scurrying down the ladder. He did not see me, but when he saw his crate was broken into he gave a deep groan. However, upon discovering the horse to be intact he became quite cheerful – not at all the manner of one who thinks he is about to die. Giving thanks to the idols of his homeland, he mounted the horse and touched a peg on its saddle. Immediately – and I implore God to strike me blind and dumb if I lie – the horse rose up into the air with the infidel sage on its back!'

Suddenly the sailor rolled up his eyes and stuck out his tongue, gurgling incomprehensibly. Caelestis gaped in amazement. Had God's curse struck him so quickly for lying?

Seeing this thought in Caelestis' eyes, the sailor burst out laughing. 'Forgive me,' he said between chuckles. 'No tale, however grim, is complete without a comic interlude. To return to events on the ship, however. I, seeing that the infidel intended to escape on his flying horse, ran forward before he could gain height and dashed out his brains with the belaying pin.

'By now the Dendan was beginning to chew the timbers in its mighty jaws. I could hear the screams of my comrades as they were cast off the deck into the sea. I lost no time in clambering onto the horse's back and pressing the peg. The horse rose up and up – out of the hold and into the sky. I looked down and it seemed as if, far below, a goldfish was nibbling at a paper toy.'

'Intriguing,' said Caelestis. 'And so you escaped. Where is the flying horse now, may I ask?'

'Ah, it was not as simple as that. For, as I circled the ship, the infidel appeared on the broken deck. My blow had sorely wounded him. As the sea rose it lapped at his robes and I saw blood in the water. Then he spoke and, though he was a mere ant from up there, I heard his voice as clearly as thunder.

'"Fly, you foreign devil!" he screamed at me. "Fly, but you will not escape my curse, which is that your wife will do you a worse wrong than infidelity and your sons a worse wrong than ingratitude—"'

The sailor paused. 'The sea swallowed him up then, so if the curse has further stipulations I do not know them. However, flying on . . .'

Caelestis held up his hand. 'Your tale is fascinating, but I'm tired and I need to sleep.

Are you familiar with the phrase "to cut a long story short"?'

The sailor was so shocked that he removed the pipe from his mouth for a few seconds. 'But I have yet to tell you of the island of singing flowers, the beautiful princess whom I wed, the return of the Yamatese sage—'

'You said he was from Khitai.'

'Er, indeed, so he was. And the story of the lovesick ghoul and the pomegranate, my second ride on the flying horse, my travails in the desert of glass, and my eventual return to Crescentium.'

Caelestis fixed him with a cynical glare, by now quite sure that the whole story was complete fiction. 'You have summed it all up admirably. And so, goodnight.'

'Wait,' said the sailor.

As Caelestis closed his eyes and lay back on the bed, he was suddenly aware of something being pressed into his hand. He looked up to see the sailor bending over him.

He found he was holding a wooden peg. 'What's this?'

'It is the peg that controls the flying horse. The thing brought me only misery, and I only wish I had drowned those many years ago. I do not know where the horse is now, but if you find it and replace this peg then it may be of some use to you.'

Caelestis didn't know what to believe. He turned the peg over in his hands. If he had still had any money he would have suspected a trick of some kind, but he had given the sailor his last coin. 'I shall keep it, thank you.'

He lay back slightly more content. Tomorrow he would find Altor and together they could search for more information about the flying horse. If it really did exist, it would be worth far more than the ring with that obstinate Faltyn.

The door of the dormitory banged open. Three soldiers of the night-watch stood there.

'Jablo the Knife,' said the sergeant. 'You're under arrest.'

THREE

IMPRISONED

Despite his protests, Caelestis was frog-marched to the city prison and flung into a cell.

'Let me out!' he yelled, hammering on the door. 'I am not Jablo.'

A panel slid open and an ugly hunchback showed his face there. 'Who are you?' demanded Caelestis.

'Your jailer. I am in charge of your well-being, but I'm afraid I don't always take my duties very seriously. Enjoy your stay.'

The hunchback snorted with laughter and closed the panel.

Caelestis screamed in pure fury. Had Fate

itself decided to conspire against him? The dormitory had been unpleasant enough, but here he was in a darkened cell with the smell of stale urine in his nostrils and only a bed of greasy straw on which to lie. High above, a narrow grating admitted a chink of moonlight.

He went to sit down, heard something rustling its way through the straw, and thought better of it. As he paced irritably up and down, tiny eyes watched him in the dim light.

'Sharing a cell with rats . . .' groaned Caelestis. 'Why didn't I just go with Altor to the monastery? Still, at least now things can't get any worse.'

The panel opened in the door. 'The time of your execution has been confirmed as one hour after dawn,' announced the hunchback.

Caelestis ran to the door. 'I'm to be hanged? But I haven't committed any crime!'

'No, no, you're not going to hang.'

Caelestis breathed a sigh of relief. 'Thank God—'

'They're going to chop your head off.' The hunchback gave a peal of laughter.

Caelestis glared at him through the narrow panel. 'If I'm to die, at least bring me a hearty meal. That's traditional, isn't it?'

'Not in my jail it isn't,' chortled the hunchback.

Caelestis shook his head wistfully as if resigned to his fate. 'All that hostility and resentment – but I understand. How you must have suffered in your life. Thrust into this world only half formed, piteously ugly and twisted, in your youth you must have been the butt of many cruel jokes. Why, even now you are forced to live a life of menial drudgery despite your obvious intelligence. No doubt the bureaucrats in charge of the prison snicker at you behind your back, imagining themselves superior. What do they know about the secret misery in your poor tormented heart? The misery of a beautiful soul trapped in a hideous body. Misery that finds its only outlet when you vent your spite on such as me.'

Tears had welled in the jailer's eyes. 'You understand! Everything you say is true, so true! But how can you, with your perfectly muscled body and fresh young features . . . How can you know what it is like for a poor hunchback like myself?'

'I will tell you the truth,' said Caelestis, with deep sincerity. 'Once I, too, was as bent and gnarled as you. Men spat on me in the street, children pelted me with rotten fruit, and dogs snapped at my heels. But I was lucky enough to fall in with a kindly old wizard from – er, well, from Khitai, actually – and he used his sorcery to transform me. No longer was I a miserable hunchback, but now the lithe and handsome youth you see before you.'

'Where can I find him?' The jailer clutched the grille. 'Tell me, I beg you. If I can find him, perhaps he'll agree to transform me as well.'

'Well, he might. He's a good friend of mine, of course. Can you read?'

'No.' The jailer's mouth drooped. 'Does that matter?'

'Not at all, but I just thought that perhaps I should write you a letter of introduction to take to the wizard. I'll explain that you're my friend. You *are* my friend, aren't you?'

'Of course.' There was a rattling noise while the jailer hurried to unlock the door. As Caelestis emerged from the cell he was engulfed in a clumsy embrace. 'How handsome I will be, thanks to you. It is a dream come true!'

'Quite so,' said Caelestis. 'Now, if you can provide me with paper and a pen . . .'

The jailer led him to a little room set aside for magistrates to sign warrants of execution. Caelestis sat at a desk and dipped his pen in the inkwell. 'You must take this letter to the commandant of the Knights Capellars, at the Temple of the Roc,' he said. 'He is a friend of mine and will lead you to the wizard.'

As the jailer skipped around out of sheer joy, Caelestis wrote:

This hunchback is an evil heretic. He is forcing me to write this on pain of torture. He thinks it is a letter of credit, but God has granted me the wisdom to outwit him.

Signed, Friar Caelestis of Cornumbria

Clutching the letter, the jailer escorted Caelestis to a postern gate of the prison and let him out into the street. 'I shall go straight away to the Capellars,' he said.

Caelestis smiled. 'See that you do, my friend.' As the jailer turned away and lurched off down the street, the smile hardened into a look of pitiless satisfaction.

Dawn was still an hour or two away, but the sky was visibly lightening. Caelestis' smile faded altogether. He was hungry, penniless and worn out – and he still had had no sleep that night.

'Next time,' he said sourly to himself, 'I shall listen to Altor.'

Altor rose as the sun pushed slim golden rays

between the carved window lattices. The pattern of light on the marble floor was like interwoven leaves. Altor rose, dressed and sat a short while in prayer before going down for breakfast.

He was directed towards the refectory by a knight who was just going off guard duty. There he found Tobias with several of his officers, discussing their military plans over a frugal meal.

Tobias looked up without smiling. 'I am pleased to see you refreshed by a good night's sleep,' he said curtly. 'Be seated and break your fast with us. You will find this plain fare more fortifying than all the overripe fruits and oily meats of the Ta'ashim lands.'

Altor looked woefully at the bread and water on the table. Though he lacked Caelestis' extravagant tastes, he had been looking forward to a rather more substantial breakfast. Nonetheless he thanked Tobias. 'I am nourished by love of Our Lord.'

A scrawny hound was crouching under the

table and looked up at Altor as he sat. Tobias coughed and ejected a gob of phlegm, which struck it between the ears. It whimpered and slunk away.

'Yon hound is like the Ta'ashim race,' grunted Tobias, with a sneer. 'It will come to beg at your table, but it is always ready to bite if you do not have the strength to show you are the master.'

Altor tore himself a chunk of bread and said nothing, more than ever convinced of Tobias' fanaticism.

Suddenly Tobias turned his ice-grey stare on him, and despite his courage Altor could not help flinching. It was like looking into the eyes of Hate. 'Well?' said Tobias flatly. 'What is your business in Crescentium?'

Altor hesitated, then drew from his haversack the hilt and jewelled pommel. 'These are fragments of the Sword of Life. The third and final part, the blade, may be somewhere in the Crusader territory or the neighbouring Ta'ashim lands—'

Tobias snorted. 'The Ta'ashim states border our own. In that sense they are neighbours, but in no other.'

'Quite so.' Altor went on: 'The blade must be found and the sword restored, as it is the only weapon that can prevail against the Five – five wizards, the last of the True Magi, who fled the destruction of the city of Spyte to become comets. In that form they have heard the music of Heaven and their powers have grown unchecked. If the Sword of Life is not made whole, the Five will return to claim this world as their own.'

Tobias rubbed his jaw. 'God has sent you to me for guidance,' he said. 'For, now I think on it, I have heard some story of this Sword of Life, and in the legends I have heard it has its dark twin, the Sword of Death. Find the one and you will find the other, is my guess. To learn more you must seek out Ormrud, a physician of Quadrille. He is the most learned man in Outremer.'

'Excellent. Where will I find him?'

'Here in Crescentium. His house is beside a fountain of black marble at the eastern end of the street of tanners.'

After breakfast, Altor went out into the street to keep his rendezvous with Caelestis. There was no sign of him. Turning to a Capellar on sentry duty at the gate, Altor said, 'I was supposed to meet my friend here. If he comes, will you tell him I have gone to the house of the physician Ormrud?'

The knight's face hardly changed under the stern prow of his helmet. 'What does your friend look like?'

'Slim, not as tall as me, very elegantly dressed. He has long black hair which he wears in a ponytail.'

'The man you are describing was arrested last night,' said the Capellar. 'By now he has been sent to meet his Maker.'

FOUR

The Healer

Much to Caelestis' disgust he had had no choice but to spend the night sleeping in one of the ramshackle slums along the side-streets leading to the bazaar, surrounded by lice-ridden beggars and stray dogs.

Even fitful slumber fled with the first light of day, and Caelestis lay glumly, eyes still closed, as the sun poked intrusive beams through the windows.

He listened to the sounds outside as the new day began: the street traders' shouts, the jangle of church bells and the caterwauling of Ta'ashim priests, the indignant braying of donkeys as they were driven to market. Every noise stabbed through Caelestis' brain. He had a splitting headache and his eyes felt like hot grit.

Beside him, the first action of the beggars as they woke was to crawl out into the street and accost passers-by with pleas for food and money. 'Give alms!' Caelestis heard the cry from outside. 'Give alms, or I am sure to starve before the dawning of a new day.'

'Get out of the way, you son of a camel,' replied a voice of fastidious disdain. 'I must get my wares to market or I will lose my investment and become as vile a pauper as yourself.'

To this discouraging tirade, the beggar replied, 'Give alms and increase your merit in the sight of God. Then you will prosper and grow rich.'

The patter did not strike Caelestis as very convincing, but it obviously worked because he heard a grudging sigh and the clink of a copper coin landing in the beggar's plate.

Caelestis realised that his clothes were

crawling with fleas. Grimacing, he got up and lurched out into the street, where he was immediately sick in the gutter.

One of the beggars looked up in irritation. 'Mongrel! Your vomit will drive away my clientele.'

Caelestis ignored him. Miserably wiping his mouth on his sleeve, he squinted through the hot sunshine to where a fountain stood at the end of the street. The cool clear water splashed invitingly across the black marble rim. Caelestis hurried across and dipped his head into the fountain, gasping at the sudden cold.

'Get away from there, you,' a woman snapped as she passed. 'You'll pollute the drinking water.'

Too dejected to think of a suitable insult, Caelestis merely hissed at her. If he had still had the ring he would have called out the Faltyn and promised it ten years of his life, whatever it asked for. Nothing could be worse than another instant in the slums of Crescentium.

Nearby, a queue of lepers and cripples stood outside a narrow, white-walled house. It looked very clean for a building right in the heart of the poor quarter. At first Caelestis refused to acknowledge anything that did not relate to his own misery, but at last curiosity got the better of him. Approaching a rug-seller on his way to market, he asked whose house it was.

'Ormrud the healer,' replied the rug-seller.

'A healer? God be praised.'

The rug-seller took this as an invitation to commence a story. 'He is said to be the wisest man in Outremer. But what is wisdom? I myself have seen—'

Caelestis was in no mood to suffer another tortuous fable. Shoving the man aside, he set off across the street with renewed hope. Even at this early hour the rising heat and dust were becoming stifling, and he was grateful for the cool shade of the entrance hall.

A young Ta'ashim woman came running up as he entered and pointed to the queue of sick people. 'These others were here before you,' she protested.

Caelestis was about to pretend that he could not understand her accent when a thin, sandy-haired man emerged from a curtained vestibule at the back of the hall. 'That's right,' said the man. 'Wealth and social rank buy no privileges here.'

'Wealth?' spluttered Caelestis. 'Social rank? I tell you truly, I am the poorest wretch in all Crescentium and therefore I deserve—'

A tall, broad-shouldered figure emerged from behind the physician. Still half dazzled by sleep and the bright sunshine outside, Caelestis blinked at him. 'Altor?'

'Caelestis!' cried Altor in delight. 'I feared you were dead.'

Caelestis fingered his dirty tunic and winced. 'Worse,' he said. 'I had to sleep rough.'

Altor roared with laughter. 'That's typical of Caelestis,' he said to Ormrud. 'Nothing upsets him as much as squalor.'

'In that case please go with Dhali,' said

Ormrud, indicating the Ta'ashim girl. 'A hot bath and a good breakfast will make a new man of you, my friend.'

As Caelestis allowed himself to be led away, Altor drew Ormrud to one side. 'Before you return to your patients, there is something I must show you.'

He drew the sword-hilt out of his haversack. In the shadowy hallway, the jewel-encrusted metal glittered like a handful of starlight.

'The Sword of Life!' gasped Ormrud. 'I thought it had been destroyed long ago.'

Altor drew it further out of the sack, then hastily tucked it away as an inquisitive patient drew near. 'The blade is still missing, as you see.'

Ormrud nodded. 'Perhaps I can help.' He ushered Altor back into the vestibule that served as his consulting room, drawing the curtain across behind them. 'There are those who would like the blade to remain undiscovered.'

'I know, but surely you don't think anyone here . . . ?'

Ormrud shrugged. 'The precaution of talking in private might be unnecessary – but why take chances? Now, let me tell you what I know. In the very earliest days of the world, as you may have heard it told, there was no way for the living and the dead to tell one another apart. Between Life and Death there was not the absolute line that exists today, but only an inconstant blur. Eventually this became intolerable – a widow does not wish to meet her dead husband while out walking with her new love, nor could anyone say who should be head of each family. So the archangel Abdiel was sent down to earth and cut apart the place that was for the living from the place for the dead. He created two icons of this parting, two great swords of power. One of these, the Sword of Death, remained beneath the world until brought back from Hades by the paladin Ganelon.'

'And the other,' said Altor, 'was the Sword of Life.'

'Quite so. It is said Ganelon hoped to use the Sword of Death against the very forces of the Devil, but was corrupted himself by the intensity of its baleful power. As to that I cannot say – I do not think that life and death are quite the same as good and evil. In any case, the Sword of Death was lost somewhere in the country that is now Marazid.'

Altor nodded impatiently. 'Yes, but it is the Sword of Life that interests me.'

'The fates of the two are inextricably linked. Yours, which contained within its blade the essence of life, was broken into three pieces by Yaunt the Seven-Eyed, a fiend from the frozen desert wastes of Krarth. I had believed even the fragments themselves were destroyed, or lost for ever beneath the ruins of Spyte. It seems that is not the case.'

Altor frowned. 'But I thought the Sword of Life was created to destroy the last of the True Magi. Wasn't it?'

'Well, not according to the version of the myth I've just told you. But remember that truth has more than one shape and speaks with more than one tongue.'

'But can it destroy them?'

'Of course,' said Ormrud, nodding. 'Blue Moon, Red Death and their ilk – they are of the undead. I mean this not in the trite sense of the term, as applied to clattering skeletons and zombies that shamble round lonely graveyards at night. Some great entities linger in this world without ever tasting death, you see. Their death is a kind of apotheosis – they become *undead*. The Five belong to this category, and the Sword of Life will sever their link with our reality and send them into the void.'

'If we can find the blade,' said Altor.

Some time later the three sat in Ormrud's private chambers. Caelestis did indeed feel a lot better now that he had bathed and Dhali had washed and mended his clothes. A nap had cured his headache, and after a wholesome meal he was no longer convinced that he was dying of food poisoning. As he nibbled at a bunch of grapes, he listened to Altor explain everything Ormrud had told him.

'So far so good,' said Caelestis. 'All we need to know now is, where exactly in Marazid is the blade located?'

'Oraba's prophecy mentioned a city beside a bay,' said Altor. 'Hakbad, perhaps?'

Caelestis spat out a pip. 'Or Kiri Umoor, or Distan, or maybe half a dozen other places.'

'Well, we have to start somewhere,' snorted Altor.

Ormrud held up his hands. 'My friends, I can only suggest that you go to see a man called Susurrien. He is an Opalarian prince, but is now exiled from the Ta'ashim lands – and with good reason. From what I hear he is as sinister as a snake. However, he is known to desire the Sword of Death for himself, and hence he may be able to give you some information about the Sword of Life.'

Caelestis jumped to his feet. Now that he was rested, he was impatient to be off. 'And where can we find this Prince Susurrien?'

'He lives here in Crescentium. But, my friends, be careful. There is a Ta'ashim proverb: "Even the lion and the serpent will lie in ambush together when both are hungry for the flesh of the gazelle." If you two are lions, Susurrien is assuredly the most venomous of serpents. He may agree to assist you, but you must never trust him.'

After being given directions, they thanked Ormrud and set out across the city, keeping to the side-streets where there was less chance of running into a militia patrol.

'Caelestis, I think you're being unduly cautious,' said Altor, as his friend ducked out of sight inside a fruit-seller's booth to avoid being seen by a magistrate lounging in a sedan chair.

'Oh yes?' Caelestis craned his neck around the awning of the booth to watch the sedan chair disappear along the street. 'You weren't the one who had to spend the night in jail. And for a crime I didn't commit!'

'That must have rankled,' laughed Altor, 'considering the number of crimes you've committed and got away with over the years.'

Caelestis was about to reply when his attention was distracted by a commotion at the end of the alley they were passing. A Ta'ashim woman in long silk robes and a veil was being molested by two red-bearded Thulander merchants.

'A damsel in distress,' said Caelestis.

'Can't have that,' agreed Altor. 'Hey, you ruffians, unhand that lady!'

The Thulanders turned, but one still held the woman in a brutish grip. 'What's the problem?' he snarled.

'Yeah,' said his friend. 'Can't a couple of guys that are new in town have a bit of fun, eh?'

'No, not if it involves manhandling this good lady,' said Altor.

The first Thulander hawked and spat. ''Od's

blood, she's just a Ta'ashim wench. Their sort doesn't count.'

'There we must disagree,' said Caelestis. He and Altor drew their swords. 'In our view, it is pigs like you that the world can do without.'

Both Thulanders wore long axes on their backs, but in the narrow alley they chose instead to draw shortswords.

'You're a stupid little runt to be insulting us,' said the one who had been holding the woman. 'Now you're going to end up without your entrails.'

'You too,' said the other man to Altor.

A sudden flash of light forced Altor and Caelestis to shield their eyes. The alley was filled with the stench of sulphur. As the yellow smoke blew away, there was no sign of the two Thulanders. Their weapons lay on the ground.

The Ta'ashim woman was standing a few paces away. By her feet were two piglets squealing indecisively. She stepped briskly forward and gathered them up, popping them into a sack that she had produced, as far as the two young friends could tell, from nowhere.

'It was very kind of you to take the trouble to help me,' she said, in an exotic lilting accent.

Altor smiled affably and sheathed his sword. Caelestis lifted his own over his head, dangled the blade straight down, and dropped it dextrously back into its scabbard. 'In the event, madam, there was no trouble,' he said, still a little unsure if he could believe what had happened.

As the woman came forward they noticed the heady scent of jasmine pervading her robes. She stepped up to Caelestis and tilted her head. Behind her veil, perhaps, she smiled. 'This unlocks the secret doors into my garden,' she said.

Caelestis was puzzled until he felt her press something into his hand and, looking down, saw a large silver key. He shrugged. 'I don't understand. Where is your garden?'

'There are many ways there, all over the

Ta'ashim world. What I say may seem baffling to you now, but listen nonetheless. If you are in need of a place to hide, then a hound will guide you to the scented garden of Fatima. Go with God.'

She bowed and swept past as silent as silk.

Caelestis looked at Altor. 'What do you think that was all about?'

Altor gave a discreet cough. On the assumption that the woman was trying to arrange an assignation with Caelestis, he had been studiedly looking the other way. 'Well . . .'

'Pah, do you really think I'm fool enough to keep a rendezvous with a Ta'ashim sorceress? Look what happened to those two.'

'So, are you going to keep that key, or throw it away?'

'It's solid silver! I'll keep it to trade with the Faltyn – Oh, no. I lost the ring.'

With all the excitement, Altor had not noticed. 'How?'

'A dice game with a bunch of sailors,' said Caelestis resentfully. 'All my money too. I'm sure they cheated, God curse them. I hope their ship sinks and they all drown.'

'I'm sure you don't mean that.' Altor looked disapprovingly at his friend, who showed, however, no sign of contrition. 'Hmmm . . . now, according to Ormrud's directions, we need to go down that street and around the next corner.'

They arrived at a butcher's shop where they had been told Susurrien had lodgings. Inside, a bearded giant of a man stood beside a marble slab on which he was dismembering a carcass. His cleaver struck the raw meat with remorseless thwacks. His eyes betrayed no emotion as he saw Altor and Caelestis enter, but the cleaver slipped, striking the stone of the slab with a metallic shriek.

He glowered at his chipped cleaver, then nodded towards the stairs.

Still no word had been spoken. Altor and Caelestis looked at each other and crossed the room. The bearded man watched them with eyes like droplets of hard resin.

'I have the strangest feeling we were expected,' said Caelestis under his breath as they began to ascend.

There was a single door at the top of the stairs. The sounds of the street outside only intensified the expectant hush. As Altor raised his fist to knock, in the shop below they heard the butcher start once more to hack at the flesh on the slab.

FIVE

The Exile

The room was plain. In a carved wooden chair like a primitive throne, a man sat at the window. He was drawing at a tall hookah that stood beside him, its bubbling the only sound in the room. The smell of scented tobacco smoke did not quite mask the stench of blood from the shop below.

Prince Susurrien turned with a rustling of stiff robes. His jewellery and gilt-decorated tunic, catching a shaft of morning sunlight, became afire with stars. The chair creaked as he shifted his body so that he was half facing his visitors. In the centre of his gold turban, a limpid red gem glowered like a third eye.

His stare was intense and unnerving. With his swarthily handsome face he looked like a man capable of great passion and cruelty. For a long moment he gazed at the two young heroes, then gestured to the cushions piled against the wall. Sharp white teeth flashed as he smiled.

Altor folded his arms and stayed where he was. Caelestis sat down on a cushion but he watched Susurrien like a cat, ready to spring up at the slightest sign of danger. From where he sat, the sunlight was behind Susurrien. Passing through the filigree screen over the window and through the dusty air, it cast across Caelestis' face a host of narrow beams, which all appeared to radiate from the exiled prince. *The spider's web* . . . thought Caelestis.

'I knew you would come,' said Susurrien, the first words he had spoken since they entered. His voice, soft and deep, suggested the quietest beat of an enormous drum.

'We are looking—' began Altor.

'You seek the Sword of Life, I the Sword of Death. By uniting we will achieve what we desire.'

Altor scowled. 'I'm not going to pretend I like the idea.'

'But we've no alternative,' interjected Caelestis. 'So, all right, what's the next step?'

Susurrien held up a little manikin that looked as if it was carved from diseased wood. 'I have here the Hatuli, literally, the "Bring-hither". It was constructed by the great wizard Saknathur, who lived five centuries past. My agents found it for me in the ruins of his fortress.'

'Very interesting,' said Altor flatly. 'How's it going to help?'

Susurrien paused before replying. If he was annoyed by Altor's tone, his steady smile betrayed none of it. 'The Hatuli has an interesting power. It can find anything that is hidden.'

'Great,' said Caelestis. 'Just tell it to find the swords and we're in business.'

'If it were operative it could locate them easily. But it is not.' He set down the manikin on the floor by his chair. There it stood waiting, lifeless. 'Its eyes are missing. They were two tiny emeralds of flawless beauty, and I believe they were prised from the Hatuli's head by Hunguk the Pirate King. It was he who slew Saknathur and ransacked his fortress.'

'So who has them now?' asked Caelestis.

Susurrien drew again on his hookah, and his smile broadened into glee. 'Hunguk still. He is immortal, and his ship now sails the seas of myth. So your quest is to steal the emeralds back from him.'

Altor fixed him with a wary glare. 'I think you're having a joke at our expense, Susurrien. *Hunguk the Pirate King* is just a story sailors tell. If there ever was such a man, he must have been dead for hundreds of years.'

'No, he is not dead – nor truly alive. Hunguk was too great a man for this world, too great to conform to its laws.'

'Too great, you say? Those are God's laws!' snapped Altor, only to catch himself sounding like mad Tobias.

Susurrien shrugged, as if Altor's beliefs were of no consequence. 'We are in the last days now, and those who are born and walk the world's face are pale in comparison with the mighty heroes of times past.'

'The great entities who linger in the world without ever tasting death,' said Altor, remembering Ormrud's words.

'Just so. I have heard it said by the scholars of your faith that Hunguk forfeited his soul for the bloody rapine he committed. They say he is doomed to roam the world till the Hour of All's Ending. I prefer to think he was too great a man for Heaven or Hell. He has sailed the only course he could – into myth.'

'Or he could be just a pile of bones on the ocean bed,' said Caelestis. 'In which case we'd be going off on a fool's errand.'

'Over the years, many have claimed to see his ship *The Devil's Runner* bearing down on them out of fog or storm. Not all can be liars.'

Susurrien allowed a few moments of silence for them to take this in, then reached for a parchment. 'I have prepared this astrological chart to show when and where *The Devil's Runner* will next appear on the earthly plane. It is a point some ninety kilometres offshore, in the Gulf of Marazid, and one day in the future. From my planisphere I know that the Swords of Life and Death are located somewhere in the city of Hakbad. Once you have recovered the emeralds, go there and seek me at the House of the Desert Breeze.'

He tossed them the chart and turned away to gaze out of the window. The audience was at an end.

Altor rolled the chart and tucked it into his belt. 'Have you any suggestions on how to get there?'

'No,' said Susurrien, in a bored tone. 'That is your problem.'

They walked in silence for a time while Altor brooded. 'I don't like it,' he said at last.

'Ha!' cried Caelestis sarcastically. 'You think you're the only one? Chasing off to sea to find an immortal pirate's magic emeralds, indeed. But what else can we do?'

'You heard what Susurrien said. The blade's in Hakbad. We could go straight there.'

Caelestis shook his head. 'It's a huge city – bigger than Tamor and Ferromaine combined, from what I hear. If we still had the Faltyn . . . But, as it is, we could spend a dozen lifetimes and still not find the blade.'

'Even so, it sticks in my craw having to trust Susurrien. Something about him made my skin crawl.'

'We don't have to trust him,' said Caelestis. 'In fact, Ormrud warned us not to. I don't think we have any choice other than to work with him for a while, but as for trust . . . Well, you're too trusting at the best of times. Better leave that side of things to me.'

Their wandering had brought them to the

outskirts of the city. Seeing a fishing village in the distance, Caelestis suggested they might walk out and enquire about hiring a sailing boat. 'Er, you do have some money left, don't you?' he added.

'Not enough. Still, let's take a look. There might be an old skiff for sale that we could patch up ourselves.'

They soon found that the village was further away than it seemed, because the track meandered between a number of low, sealed stone buildings. Time wore on towards midday and the heat soared. Dry dust rose chokingly from the road as they walked.

Turning a bend, they came across a man of Coradian stock sitting by the roadside drinking from a gourd. As he tilted it to his mouth, cool wine splashed in the sunlight. At the sight of this, Caelestis licked his dry lips enviously.

The man noticed them and smiled. 'We must swelter in the sun while those who lie in these tombs enjoy the cool shade. But they must endure their parched throats, as this wine is only for the living.' He offered the gourd. 'Join me?'

Caelestis needed no further invitation. He sat on a pile of stones and took a long swig from the gourd. The wine was delicious.

'Have you come far?' asked the man, mopping his sunburnt brow.

'From Crescentium.'

'And going far?'

Caelestis took another gulp before passing the gourd to Altor. 'Only to the fishing village yonder.'

Altor, in a suspicious mood after their meeting with Susurrien and fearing that his friend might blurt out the details of their quest, hurriedly changed the subject. 'These strange buildings around us are mausoleums then?'

'Indeed. This is where the Ta'ashim notables buried their dead in the days before our forerunners came from the north to conquer Outremer.'

'I thought you weren't Ta'ashim yourself,' said Caelestis, nodding. He got the gourd back from Altor and took another swig.

'I'm from Krarth originally,' said the man.

Altor gave him a searching look. 'Ah, yes, that's the accent. And where are you travelling?'

He shrugged. 'In neither one direction nor the other. I sit here in a company of three – I, my shadow and my memories. My companions are not quarrelsome, and in this life that is as much as one can ask for.'

'Admirable sentiments,' said Altor. 'Still, time is pressing and we must be on our way.' He took the gourd out of Caelestis' hands and gave it back to the man.

Caelestis cast a weary glance towards the village. For all their walking it still seemed no nearer. 'The thing of it is,' he confided suddenly, ignoring the scathing look he got from Altor, 'we have to rendezvous with a certain vessel ninety kilometres out in the Gulf of Marazid. We must find a way to be there tomorrow.'

The man whistled through his teeth. 'How fortunate that you mentioned this to me, for I truly believe your quest would have been doomed to failure if you had not. You see, it is well-known that at this time of year the Gulf is frequented by a gargantuan sea monster called the Dendan. The local fishermen are in fear, and cling to the shore as a babe to its mother's breast. You would never have found anyone willing to lend you his boat for such a venture.'

'In that case—' began Caelestis.

'Excuse us,' said Altor. He grabbed Caelestis by the arm and dragged him off to one side. 'What are you playing at?'

'Eh?'

'See if this phrase rings any bells: "You're too trusting at the best of times." I'm too trusting? So how come you're telling this guy everything?'

'He mentioned the Dendan. That bit's genuine. Let's see what he has to say, anyway.'

'Let's not!'

'Just because he's from Krarth you think he must be an agent of the Five Magi. I'm surprised at you, Altor.'

The man came over and extended his hand. 'I realise we haven't been introduced. I'm Galor the tomb robber.'

Altor stared at him. 'You admit to plundering these tombs?'

Galor smiled sheepishly. 'They're Ta'ashim. We stole their whole country.'

The heat, wine and lingering fatigue from the night before had all conspired to unfocus Caelestis' thoughts. 'Tomb robbing is not necessarily the vilest of crimes,' he announced.

Altor scowled at them both. Seeing he had nothing to say, Galor went on: 'But listen now, because I can help you in your quest. I was sitting here a few days ago when I was taken by an urge to have gulls' eggs for my supper. There are none to be found in the necropolis, of course, so I went up there to see if any gulls were nesting in the hillside.' He pointed to a steep path beyond the tombs.

'Gulls' eggs,' said Caelestis dreamily. 'Scrambled, with coriander and thyme seasoning, served on toasted muffins with a sprig of parsley . . .'

'My friend, what I found was the mother of all eggs,' said Galor, breaking Caelestis' reverie, 'for I discovered a great marvel. Up there is a cave where the fabled Roc has its nest.'

'A nest of rocks?' said Altor impatiently. 'Absurd!'

'Ah, you do not know the Ta'ashim legends. The Roc is a giant bird which the mariner Simbar encountered on one of his voyages. He used it to invade the inviolable citadel of Shazireh the witch by tying himself to its claw while it slept. When the Roc took to the air, it carried Simbar aloft with it.'

'And you suggest we should try the same trick.' Altor nodded. 'I see. Well, Galor—'

'Oh no, young sir. I'm not suggesting that at all. I just thought you might want to steal the Roc's egg, which you could sell in

Crescentium and hire a ship strong enough to withstand the sea monsters of the Gulf.'

Altor was taken aback. 'So, you're not proposing we should tie ourselves to the Roc's claw like Simbar?'

Galor laughed. 'How would you make the bird land at the right spot? No, it would be suicide.'

'Too right!' declared Caelestis, with feeling.

But Altor, now that he no longer felt he was being made to go along with the scheme, had started to give it serious consideration. 'We could make reins,' he said, 'and ride the giant bird to our rendezvous. I'm a good horseman.'

'Horses,' pointed out Caelestis, 'only leave the ground for a few seconds at a time.'

'Why don't I show you the Roc's nest anyway?' suggested Galor. 'I know a route where we can get quite close without being seen. If you decide then that the prospect of flying on its back is too daunting, well, at least you'll have a tale to tell your grandchildren.'

Caelestis waved his hand expansively. 'Why not? Looking can't do any harm. Lead the way, Galor.'

Galor took them up into the hills. In was a hard climb, doubly wearying in the baking heat of the afternoon. By the time they reached level ground and turned to look back the way they'd come, Caelestis and Galor between them had finished the gourd of wine. Altor remained thirsty, preferring to keep a clear head even if it meant a dry tongue.

From here the tombs were tiny heaps of pebbles, the bay a silver-blue mirror whose glare made the distant rooftops of Crescentium shimmer like a mirage.

Galor pointed to a wide shelf of rock in front of a cave. 'That's where we have to go.'

They sidled along a tortuous ledge, Galor showing no fear despite the sheer drop below. To Caelestis, as sure-footed as a goat, it was no more worrying than a stroll along the street. Only Altor was careful not to look down.

They reached the cave entrance. The sun made the rocks around them as hot as a furnace, but the interior of the cave exuded a dank chill.

'Is this it?' said Caelestis, stepping down off the ledge. 'We'll be able to see the Roc's nest from here?'

'Ssh,' said Altor. 'We don't want to disturb it.'

'Too late for that!' cried Galor in sudden glee. 'Fools! This very cave is the Roc's eyrie! I have brought you to your doom.'

And from the depths of the cave came the harsh shriek of a giant bird of prey.

SIX

Green Flame

Galor had something in his hand: a green glass globe. He was about to throw it down, but before he could do so Caelestis grabbed his arm. The two swung round, grappling off balance on the brink of the ledge. The glass globe slipped from Galor's hand and fell. It cracked and liquid green flames spread across the rock, cutting off any hope of retreat the way they had come.

Galor stopped struggling with Caelestis and stared in horror. 'No . . .' he gasped. 'Now I'm trapped here too.'

'It serves you right. It was the fate you intended for us.'

Something huge was moving towards the cave entrance. Both Altor and Caelestis drew their swords and backed to the far side of the ledge, away from the barrier of green flame.

'What is it, Galor?' said Caelestis. 'The Roc?'

Galor huddled down on the ledge, his muscles slack with sheer terror. He looked as if he was trying to make himself so small and insignificant that the creature wouldn't notice him.

'Just one question,' growled Altor. 'Why?'

'My master, Green Flame, commanded it,' said Galor, trembling.

Caelestis looked at Altor. 'About people from Krarth, you were right. In future we will *not* trust them.'

Galor was gazing into the darkness that filled the interior of the cave. Loud scratchings and rustlings reverberated out of the depths. White with dread, Galor seemed as if terror had put him into a trance. 'It was while I slept,' he muttered. 'I saw his face in the northern lights and he told me what I must do. In a tomb, as he directed, I found that magic globe and a map that showed where the Roc had its eyrie. But now the globe is broken . . .' He cast a sidelong glance at the wall of leaping flames. 'He said it would trap you. It has trapped me too.'

Caelestis took a step towards the flames, but the heat was too intense. He looked back at Altor and shook his head. 'We'd be burned to a crisp.'

'Too late anyway. Here it comes,' said Altor. He set himself in the middle of the ledge, his silver sword glimmering green in the eldritch firelight.

It came with a screech to freeze the blood. With a beak like a warship's prow, glaring eyes like burnished shields, talons that could crush a horse, the Roc erupted from its lair to face them.

Its eyes swept across the ledge. Caelestis and Altor had never felt anything like the merciless icy intensity of that gaze. For an instant they felt as if the Angel of Death himself had turned to take notice of them.

Then Caelestis realised something. It was not only mindless ferocity that he saw in those terrifying eyes, but confusion and pain. Emerging suddenly from its gloomy cavern into the blistering daylight of mid-afternoon, the Roc was blinded.

Caelestis' sword touched a rock outcropping as he edged sideways. Instantly the giant bird swung its head to face him. The ruff of feathers around its neck bristled and it opened its beak to give vent to another petrifying screech.

It was poised to strike. Caelestis had to act at once. He dived to one side, at the same time throwing his voice so that it seemed as if Galor had cried out in fear.

The Roc snapped its gaze around to where Galor cowered. A wing swept out, as huge and swift and unstoppable as a ship's boom. Then Galor was gone, and they did not hear even a cry as he fell.

Altor stepped forward and thrust his sword towards the Roc's neck, hoping to impale it with one strong blow, but it jerked back its head so that he barely drew blood. Lashing out again, it buffeted him aside and he staggered to the very lip of the ledge. For a moment he teetered over the side and had a sickening view hundreds of metres straight down. Galor lay far below, a tiny smear of red on the sharp grey rocks.

Altor's free hand shot out and by luck found a jutting rock to hold on to. He swung himself back to safety. The Roc stared madly back at him and, for an instant, he was reminded again of the fanatic gaze of Tobias. Altor smiled, knowing that once the Roc's vision cleared he would be smiling in the face of Death.

Caelestis was beside the barrier of flames. The heat singed his clothes. He could see from Altor's attack that weapons would be useless against such a gigantic foe.

'Here I am!' he bellowed, at the top of his lungs. 'Come and get me!'

The Roc jabbed its beak towards him. For a split second Caelestis stood transfixed as he saw it shooting towards him, then at the last moment he flung himself flat. The Roc's head disappeared into the wall of fire.

There was a shriek that sounded like the sky tearing in half. Pounding its claws, huge wings beating in panic, the Roc writhed to and fro across the ledge. Flames engulfed its head and the air was choking with the stench of burning flesh and feathers.

Blindly it lashed out towards Altor. The only way he could avoid being crushed by the talons was to catch hold of the creature's leg. He realised his mistake a moment later when the Roc launched itself off into space.

Caelestis jumped, grabbing the Roc's tail feathers, and the two were carried off the ledge.

The Roc fell, a plume of sparks and smoke streaming from its burning head. The cliff rushed past, jagged razors of rock leapt up.

Caelestis and Altor both shouted in alarm and held on for grim death.

They feared the Roc was too badly wounded to fly, but then it spread its wings and with slow powerful beats rose up into the sky.

Above was an ice-blue bowl in which the sun burned bright gold. The clouds looked close enough to touch. As the wind whipped by, the two heroes caught their breath and looked down to see the coast pass beneath them. Tiny figures pointed up and seemed to be shouting, but the two friends were too high up to hear what they were saying. Caelestis and Altor could barely hear each other.

'We've got to let go!' called Caelestis.

Altor cast a glum look down at the sea. He feared no foe to which he could hold a weapon, but heights were another matter.

'Altor,' Caelestis insisted, 'we've got to let go now, before we get too far out from the coast.'

Altor shook his head. He knew Caelestis was right but his arms and legs, wrapped tightly around the Roc's leg, refused to budge. 'You'd better go without me,' he said through chattering teeth.

Caelestis was not having that. He had no intention of letting Altor sacrifice himself. Dropping his sword, he used his free hand to swing down from the giant bird's tail feathers towards the leg where Altor clung.

The Roc, incensed by pain and panic, shook its legs furiously. Caelestis slipped, but caught a fistful of feathers and climbed round towards Altor.

'I can't let go,' said Altor. He managed a sheepish grin.

'First of all, let me have that.' Caelestis took the sword out of his hand and sheathed it.

'Why did you do that?'

'Because I didn't want you to drop it in the sea.'

Caelestis took a firm grip on the Roc's leg with his left hand, braced his feet on its claws, and swung his right fist solidly into the middle of his friend's face.

Altor was a strong young man – stronger than many a warrior in his prime – and Caelestis could never have knocked him out. But the shock of the blow alone was enough to loosen his grip. 'Ow,' he said, with a comical frown, as he plummeted down towards the sea.

Caelestis jumped after him. As he fell, he cast a last look up at the Roc, which flew like a blazing comet out to sea. Then the water came rushing up and slammed the life out of him.

Caelestis was dreaming about a beautiful maiden, one of the houris who welcomed the faithful into the Ta'ashim paradise. Finding Caelestis borne into the afterlife on a golden barge, having died a doubtless heroic death, she bent to revive him with a long lingering kiss.

The kiss tasted of saltwater. And the houri had coarse bristles on her chin. Deciding he didn't much care for paradise, Caelestis opened his eyes to find Altor about to give him mouth-to-mouth.

'You can keep your lips to yourself, thanks very much,' he said grumpily.

'Fine.' Altor sat down on the sand beside him. 'Sorry I couldn't find a pretty girl to do the job.'

'Oh God, I've broken my back.' Caelestis sat up. 'Well, perhaps not. But it feels like it. And all my other bones too.'

A crowd was gathering from the local fishing village. 'Did you see that big bird?' said a child.

'That was the Roc, son,' said the boy's father.

'See it?' said Caelestis, holding up a feather as long as his arm. 'We were clinging to it.'

There was a gasp from the villagers. 'That's amazing!' said a man with ears like cauliflowers. 'A Roc's feather. How much do you want for it?'

Altor got wearily to his feet. 'We nearly

drowned, and you want to start bargaining for a feather.'

Caelestis bounded to his feet, all aches quite forgotten, and went over to the man. 'Now, your name is . . . ?'

'I am Wuraq, the son of Abdalla the net-maker.'

'Wuraq, do you own a fishing boat?'

'Certainly.'

'Well, this feather is obviously worth a great deal. It's almost unique, after all. You could get a tidy sum for it in Crescentium market . . .'

'You want to exchange it for my boat? By all means.'

Caelestis handed over the feather with a frown. He distrusted any deal made so readily.

'We should set sail without delay,' said Altor.

Wuraq said nothing but looked along the beach, preoccupied.

They followed him towards the village,

with the other fisherfolk and a horde of scrawny children, brown as nuts, who plucked at their clothes and screeched for presents.

Altor scowled at them, relented and reached into his money pouch. He held out his hand to the nearest child, who was astonished when a heavy coin dropped in the sand at his feet. The din stopped as the children all stared in disbelief at the glittering silver florin.

'Now, be off with you, eh?' said Altor, but not unkindly.

The silence lasted just a second; then, as one, the crowd came to life. Snatching up the coin, the child gave a delighted yell and tore off down the beach with his friends at his heels, tossing the coin into the air and catching it. Altor watched with a smile, seeing the way the little faces lit up when the sunlight glanced off the spinning coin.

'Oh, give away our money by all means,' said Caelestis, sarcastically.

Before Altor could reply, another voice

said: 'The Father of All sees your kindness and will reward you for it.'

They turned. Beside them stood an old and gnarled Ta'ashim woman. 'This is my grandmother,' said Wuraq. 'They are very generous, Grandmother. See this magnificent feather? They gave it to me in exchange for my boat.'

'We need to sail out into the Gulf of Marazid,' said Altor.

Eyes flashing, the old woman glared at Wuraq and began to berate him in the Ta'ashim tongue. He merely stood listening, now and then giving a stubborn shake of his head. Suddenly she made a grab for the feather. Wuraq snatched it away, both tugged for a few seconds, and the quill broke. There were a few seconds' silence while everyone stared at the ruined Roc's feather – in perfect condition a priceless treasure, but now worth not so much as a copper penny.

The old lady turned to Altor and Caelestis.

'My shiftless grandson has cheated you! *There* is his boat!'

She stabbed her finger down the shore and they turned to see what vessel they had bought.

'I don't see any boat,' said Caelestis, puzzled. 'There's just that pile of rotting driftwood . . .'

And then it dawned on him. The pile of driftwood was their boat.

SEVEN

The Horse

Sunset drenched the coast in a welter of black and red, but the darkness did not last long. Soon a full moon rose, bright as a silver coin. The sea lay still, a sheet of black onyx rippled with slow phosphorescent waves.

Caelestis hurled a pebble into the water in frustration. 'According to Susurrien's chart we have less than twenty-four hours to reach the place where *The Devil's Runner* will appear. Even if we were given the best yacht in the Middle East, and a crew of expert sailors to man her, we still couldn't make it.'

Altor sighed. 'We'll have to go back to Susurrien—'

'He won't be there. He's on his way to Hakbad by now.'

'Well, then, we'll seek him out in Hakbad and think of some other way to find the swords.'

Footsteps in the soft sand made them turn. It was Wuraq. 'You've got a nerve, showing your face,' snorted Caelestis.

Wuraq had the decency to look ashamed. 'I am sorry. What can I say? Greed got the better of me – I thought I could sell the Roc's feather and never have to work again. But God has meted out a just punishment. The feather is broken and worthless.'

'If we hadn't been in such a hurry we could have sold it ourselves,' moaned Caelestis, hardly listening to what Wuraq had to say. 'Right now we could have had a ship of our own and be sailing to our rendezvous. Instead of which we're stuck out here on the beach with nowhere to sleep.'

Wuraq wrung his hands. 'Well, that was what my grandmother . . . I came to invite you, if you want, to spend the night at our cottage.'

'Hah!' Caelestis stared at him in cold fury. 'How much will it cost us? Both our noses and Altor's magic sword?'

'No, no, my friend. I wish to make honest redress for my misdeeds. Please, come in and have supper with us, at least.'

Caelestis was annoyed, certainly, but he was also ravenously hungry and allowed himself to be led into the cottage. There the old lady, who gave her name as Menira, handed out little cups of hot, dark coffee. The smells of fish stew and baked bread rose from the stove.

The cottage had few furnishings, but Wuraq found a couple of rugs for then to sit on. 'As you see, I am a poor man,' he said.

'No poorer than we,' muttered Caelestis, under his breath.

Not wishing to offend Menira with a show of bad manners, Altor nodded to a rug that hung across the back of the room, partitioning off the rear of the cottage. 'A fine tapestry, madam,' he said. 'Your own work?'

It showed a horse bounding across clouds and sea. Menira smiled and shook her head. 'My daughter made that, God rest her soul, basing it on stories of Ridaq's flying horse.'

'A flying horse?' said Caelestis, remembering the sailor's tale he'd heard at Alexius' the night before.

'Indeed!' Wuraq leapt to his feet and drew back the rug. There, in the room beyond, was a life-size effigy of a horse made of ebony and ivory.

'A very fine work of art,' said Altor approvingly.

'More than that . . .' Caelestis got slowly to his feet. He stared at the horse open-mouthed, then he approached and ran his hands over the smooth neck, the intricately carved locks of the mane. Yes, sure enough, there was a slot at the base of the neck.

Caelestis rummaged in his pocket and brought out the peg. It fitted perfectly.

Wuraq stood by, looking puzzled, but Menira flung up her hands with amazement. 'Patience is more bitter than coffee,' she said, 'but bears a fruit sweeter than figs. I have waited my whole life for someone to come with the peg that brings to life the magic horse.'

'That's surprising,' said Caelestis. 'The sailor told me—'

'What sailor?' said Altor. 'Where did you get that peg?'

Caelestis resented his friend's tone. 'It was fairly and squarely paid for.' To Menira he said: 'How long have you had this horse?'

'It was carved by my own grandfather, whose name was Ridaq. When the Sultan held a contest among the craftsmen of the city, my grandfather was inspired to produce this marvel, a flying horse, carved of ebony and inlaid with ivory panels. At first the Sultan did not believe the astounding story my grandfather told, for who would credit a living horse that could fly, much less a wooden one? He thought my grandfather was being insolent, and had him thrown into prison. But later the Sultan's son experimented with the horse and undertook a thrilling journey to a land beyond Khitai. There he rescued a princess who had been imprisoned by her evil uncle, and he brought her back to Crescentium to wed her. My grandfather was set free and given a robe of honour, and the horse was returned to him.'

'Intriguing,' said Caelestis, shaking his head at the wonder of it all. 'Still, how did the peg come to be lost?'

'The Sultan's son wore it as a keepsake on a thong around his neck, so I am told. It must have remained in the royal family and been lost when they fled Crescentium.'

'When you northerners came,' said Wuraq.

'But . . . in that case . . .' Caelestis sighed,

close to exasperation. 'How can that be? The sailor must have been lying – and yet how did he come by the peg?'

'I always thought that was just a story,' said Wuraq. 'But it's true, then? The horse really can fly?'

Caelestis twisted the peg a few millimetres and the horse rose a metre or so into the air.

'We'd better not put it to the test now,' said Altor. 'It's dark, and we're all tired. Let's wait until morning.'

While Wuraq and his grandmother slept, Caelestis sat up and stared into the dying red embers of the fire. He could not help brooding about the peg. He had got it so cheaply because the sailor said the horse had brought him enough misery already. But if the sailor's story had not been true, it cast doubt also on his motives for selling the peg . . . Caelestis' brow furrowed. It was all very confusing.

Altor came and sat beside him. 'Can't sleep either,' he said with a yawn.

For a while they sat in silence. 'It's been quite a day,' said Caelestis, 'even for us.'

'Yes. I wondered how long it would take the Magi to get onto us.'

'Only Green Flame so far. He's usually the first to play his hand.'

'Except for Blue Moon, who's often so subtle that you don't notice what he's done until it's too late.'

They were both smiling. 'Listen to us,' said Caelestis. 'Six months of adventuring and we think we're the world's experts.'

'Yes. Caelestis, this horse is just what we need, but . . .'

'But what?'

'We can't possibly pay them what it's worth. A flying horse – *and* it's an old family heirloom.'

'If Wuraq hadn't ruined the Roc's feather that would have been a fair exchange.'

'Hardly. And perhaps they don't want to sell it.'

Caelestis clicked his tongue. He looked

at the horse, still hovering silently in the shadows at the back of the cottage. The firelight splashed along its ebony flanks, and made gleaming amber of the ivory hoofs and teeth and eyes.

Off to one side, Menira and her grandson snored contentedly, fast asleep.

'I know what you're thinking,' said Altor. 'No.'

'It's one act of theft balanced against the fate of the world.'

'Caelestis, we cannot save the world by sinning. Heroes' actions should never be unjust.'

'Heroes? We're two youths on a quest too big for us. Tell me which is more important: that we find the Sword of Life, or avoid upsetting Menira and Wuraq?'

'I don't want to make that kind of choice.'

'Maybe it's the kind of choice that heroes have to make. If the only decisions were easy ones then anyone could be a hero. In any case, I can tell that, deep down, you've already made up your mind to steal it.'

'How is that?'

'Because you're still whispering.'

That stopped Altor in his tracks. For a young monk with high ideals, it was not pleasant to face up to unworthy thoughts. After a moment's thought, he crossed himself. Speaking quite loudly, he said: 'I pray that God will forgive me if, even for a second, I considered committing any sin.'

Menira raised her head. 'I'm sorry if I woke you,' said Altor.

'I was already awake. I hope you don't mind, but I overheard what you were saying. I can't pretend to understand all of it, but I know you need the horse for something important. Of course you must take it.'

Abashed that Menira had heard him planning to rob her, Caelestis said: 'A flying horse is a great treasure. We would pay you if we could.'

'Once you have flown off on the horse,' said Menira lightly, 'the news will soon spread and people will come from far away to hear the story and look at my daughter's tapestry – and they'll pay. So I'll have my reward.'

'Excellent,' said Altor. 'This is an arrangement that suits everyone. You see, Caelestis, virtue is always rewarded. Now that's settled, I think I'll get some sleep.'

Where the mountains met the night sky, a sinister figure in robes and armour of half a world away stood looking down at the village where Altor and Caelestis slept.

'In my country there is a saying,' he murmured, more to himself than to the man who stood beside him. '"The soundest slumber comes on the day before one dies."'

The other man stepped forward, a Ta'ashim sailor in ragged clothes. For a long time they had gazed down without a word, with only the wind and the moonlight for company. The loneliness of the spot had made the sailor uneasy. He took the other's words as an invitation to speak. 'Have I not served you well, master?'

The other man slowly turned his head, as though to look at an insect. 'You have done as I told you. If you had not, then you would already be dead.'

The Ta'ashim smiled. To cover his nervousness, he sucked at the pipe he always carried, though it was not lit. 'I gave him the peg, master. Just as you said.'

'By now they will surely have bought the horse – or stolen it, more likely. Tomorrow it will fly them to their rendezvous. It will be a ride with no returning.'

'There is one thing, master . . .' The Ta'ashim sailor hesitated under the lambent scrutiny of those cruel almond-shaped eyes. The silence grew too uncomfortable to bear, so he went on. 'How did you know where they'd be? And that they'd find the horse?'

The other took from his belt a silver bottle chased with finely wrought runes. 'I had three glimpses of the future, three questions answered by a dead man.'

The Ta'ashim bit on his pipe to keep his

teeth from chattering. If not for the sheer drop behind him he would have backed away.

'Those answers served me in good stead,' went on the warlock, 'but they were not enough. Now I need three more . . .'

The curved blade was in his other hand, but by the time the sailor saw it, his heart had already been pierced.

EIGHT

The Devil's Runner

'Astounding,' said Caelestis, looking down at Altor.

Altor wore a dubious frown as he watched the horse bobbing up and down in the air. 'The peg makes it go up and down, but what about steering?'

'I just use my legs – see?' Caelestis made the horse perform a slightly shaky figure of eight, then twisted the peg to bring himself down to the beach. 'It's just like riding.'

'Except not on terra firma.'

Caelestis laughed. 'You were keen enough to put reins on the Roc, as I remember. It's a bit different when faced with the reality of flying, eh?'

'I am no coward,' retorted Altor, nettled. 'I merely think that if God had intended us to fly he would have—'

Caelestis held up his hand. 'Please. I suspect that in future times that will become a cliché, and in any case this flying horse is what Providence has seen fit to provide. Don't look it in the mouth!'

Although the hour was early, a crowd of astonished fisherfolk had gathered at the top of the beach to watch. Everyone was too much in awe to come close. Wuraq strode up and down, beaming with self-importance, telling anyone who would listen the tale of his great-great-grandfather.

Menira hobbled over. 'I suppose you'll be anxious to leave,' she said.

Altor looked from her to the horse and gave an uneasy smile. 'Caelestis is anxious to leave; I am merely anxious.'

As Altor mounted behind him, Caelestis

said: 'Once more I have to thank you for your hospitality, Menira. When I think of what I said last night, it makes me quite ashamed.'

She shook her head. 'In my old age I have learned to recognise goodness when it is present in people's hearts. I see it in you. May the peace, safety and success that are granted by the Maker of All Things fall to you in abundance.'

'And may He bless you for your kindness,' said Altor.

Caelestis touched the peg again and the horse soared up into the air.

The crowd gasped and stared. As the horse dwindled to a speck in the sky, Wuraq spoke to his grandmother. 'Will we ever see them again?'

'Who knows?' she said, shielding her eyes from the bright morning sun. 'We can only hope that the horse brings them more luck than it did your great-great-grandfather.'

Caelestis could not resist making a long

sweeping circuit of the bay before heading out to sea. 'Look at the city!' he cried to Altor. 'The buildings are just like toys. And see those people streaming to market? Don't they remind you of ants?'

'Um,' was all Altor would say. He kept a firm grip on the cantle at the back of the saddle and was staring steadfastly ahead.

'This is better than Augustus' carpet,' Caelestis said appreciatively as he veered the horse to the south-west.

'I'd have to agree with you. If one has to fly, it's better not to be flown by a madman.'

The sea, whipping past below, was a painter's palette of grey and blue. Suddenly dipping the horse, Caelestis took them down in a steep dive that made Altor's stomach churn. At the last moment he pulled up on the magic peg, so that the horse levelled out and flew along just skimming the waves.

'Then again . . .' said Altor queasily.

'Is that better?' Caelestis called over his shoulder. 'I know you don't like heights.'

Altor looked at the water shooting past just metres below. He glanced back the way they had come. Already there was no sight of land. 'It's difficult to say if it's any better,' he said. 'It's no worse. Either way, if the magic runs out we drown, but at least here we cut out the fall beforehand.'

They flew on for hours while the sun climbed to its zenith and slowly began to slide down into the west. The day would have been blazing hot, but the air whipped at their clothes and swept cool gusts into their lungs. By late afternoon the glare from the sea had given them raw red faces and its constant rolling made them feel sick, but they were exhilarated at the sight of an island ahead.

Caelestis slowed the horse to hover while Altor consulted the astrological chart Susurrien had given them.

'I think we're looking for an island,' said Altor, struggling to read the chart while the sea breeze tried to tear it from him. 'There's a note that says – oh, blast it! Where . . . ah, yes, it says, *Isle of Sunset.*'

Caelestis nudged the horse over to the island. They touched down on a shore of coral-pink sand. Bare black rocks rose towards the centre, which seemed barren of life.

'Is this the Isle of Sunset?' Altor wondered. 'There's nothing else marked anywhere near.'

'Well, I made sure to get my bearings when we took off, and we've been going in a dead straight line. So, unless Susurrien was lying, this must be the place. How long have we got?'

'The note on the chart says: *At the velvet hour the ship shall appear.* Which I take to mean between sunset and moonrise, Susurrien obviously having a poetic bent.'

'A sure sign of villainy,' laughed Caelestis, dismounting.

The sand crunched underfoot like tiny crystals of salt. Dead seaweed lay in tangled brown strands. Apart from the lapping of the waves there was no sound.

'Look at this.' Altor jumped down from the

saddle, relieved to be back on dry land. He bent to pick up something that gleamed like old ivory. The upper part of a skull.

'Some poor wretch must have been shipwrecked here,' said Caelestis. 'What a miserable place to be stranded.'

The sun declined further in the sky. As it touched the clifftops, the shadows turned the shore dark like blood. Altor and Caelestis were both gripped by a sense of impending destiny. They stood in awestruck silence as a thick bank of mist rolled in around the island. It was like being caught by the smoky exhalation of a slumbering ice-dragon.

Altor stood peering out to sea. Where only minutes before they had had a clear view as far as the horizon, now it felt as if the little island had been closed off from the rest of the world – as if the mist had cut them adrift from reality and placed them halfway into limbo.

Caelestis thought he sensed a deep vibration in the ground. Touching a rock, he felt it tremble under his fingertips. A sound too low for human hearing was rumbling through the bedrock of the island.

The dank air seemed electrified. Silent pulses of violet-blue light flickered in the fog.

'It's here,' said Altor.

Caelestis turned to look. Against the luminous backdrop of mist, a ship loomed as big as a castle. Immense and unstoppable, it slid past slowly as they watched.

Altor was the first to come to his senses. Rushing to the horse, he leapt into the saddle. 'Quick, Cael,' he said. 'We have only a few minutes before the ship leaves this world.'

Caelestis placed his hand on the horse's back and vaulted up behind his friend. 'Don't you want me to steer?'

'I'm sure I can manage.' Altor grinned. He had not much enjoyed the flight across the sea, but with the prospect of action he was himself again. Turning the peg, he caused the horse to shoot out across the water at breakneck speed. Another twist gave height, bringing them level with the high rail of *The Devil's Runner.*

Altor glided down rapidly to land on the deck. In an instant he was out of the saddle, sword in hand.

'Steady,' said Caelestis, swinging down. 'I can't see any enemies yet.'

It was true. The deck seemed deserted. With the fog drifting in tendrils between its colossal masts, the ship seemed to hang in a space between worlds. Glancing down, they could no longer make out the surface of the ocean or even hear the waves lapping against the hull.

There was one thing to be heard in the eerie calm. Intermittent moans came from far away, snatches of disembodied sound, like the cries of all the sailors ever lost at sea.

Shaking off such thoughts, they began to explore the deck. The ship was even bigger than they had first thought – bigger by far than the largest of the Crusader vessels, which could each hold a thousand men. Masts clad in plates of bronze rose up until their tops faded into the fog. The sails, cobweb sheets of mouldered canvas, hung in great swathes like the foliage of a rainforest.

'It is a fortress afloat,' said Altor.

'Then where are the sentries?' said Caelestis.

They came to a companionway whose opening was adorned with scowling demonic carvings. It seemed to lead to the bowels of the ship. Just as they were about to venture below, Caelestis caught Altor's arm.

'Look,' he said.

Up on the bridge, standing rigid at the wheel, was a figure wreathed in a long black cape. He was so still that at first they had just taken him for a scrap of tattered canvas.

With Altor leading the way, they climbed the steps to the bridge. Altor paused as he neared the top, where he could still jump down to the quarterdeck in case of attack. But the figure stood unmoving, white hands resting on the wheel.

'Is it Hunguk?' called up Caelestis.

Altor peered through the fog, then wished he hadn't. The figure's cheeks were hard and pale and he seemed to wear a disquietingly fixed grin.

'Are you Hunguk?' he said.

'Hunguk the Pirate King? Not I!' The voice was gusty and grey, a voice of storm-tossed seas and cold nights under lashing rain. 'Hunguk's not aboard. I'm Shambeer, his trusty steersman. None more trusty than I. See this wheel? My old hands haven't left this wheel in seven mortal lifetimes. "Outlived his own flesh in Hunguk's service" – that's what they say of old Shambeer.'

Under the long coat, thin shoulders twitched in a silent laugh.

'Ask him where Hunguk is,' said Caelestis, from behind Altor's shoulder.

'Where—?'

'I heard, lad. I'm not so deaf as earless-looking. Why d'you want to know?'

'Er . . . we were thinking of signing on.'

Shambeer fixed him with a disturbingly

hollow gaze. '*Nobody* signs on, lad. Not these days. The navigator's gone, and blind Destiny now plots our course. So my advice to you is scurry back where you came. And be quick about it. *The Devil's Runner* will tarry on this mortal plane but a scant few minutes, and when we leave, our destination is Eternity.'

Before Altor could reply, Caelestis leaned forward and said, 'We'll do just that, good sir. And thank you for your advice.'

Suddenly Shambeer snapped his jaws and jerked his head to stare off into the fog. 'Caligosums and luridors! They're all about us! Be off, you two, for if I'm distracted now then Satan's sharks will have our bones to gnaw on.'

Altor and Caelestis returned to the main deck. Altor glanced back at the steersman, who was now whirling the wheel to and fro with alacrity. 'I don't know what he can see in the fog, but it's keeping him occupied.'

Caelestis nodded. 'Good. Now's our chance to find those emeralds. Hunguk's cabin is the place to start.'

He stepped cautiously down the companionway. A little light trickled up from below, and in it he could see that he was in a passage. The air was thick and musty, but at least it was warmer below decks than in the white mist above.

Altor joined him, running his hand across the mahogany panels of the wall. 'These carvings are antique,' he said. 'This ship could have been afloat a thousand years!'

'I don't doubt it.' Caelestis pointed off down the passage, towards the faint light. 'Let's get a move on. I don't relish getting caught by the Pirate King.'

They came to what seemed to be the crew's quarters. Light, pallid and flickering, came from opalescent globes set into the bulkhead. It was a vast space, with bunks for at least a thousand men stretching the whole length of the ship, but, all the same, the low ceiling and long wavering shadows gave the pair a sense of claustrophobia.

There was no sign of any living soul. The

few occupied bunks contained only skeletons clothed in dust and rags.

Looking round, Caelestis backed into one of the bunks. A skeletal hand dropped, brushing his hair, and he jumped in alarm. But the arm only hung there, lifeless.

'What we're looking for won't be here,' said Altor grimly. 'The captain's cabin ought to be at the stern.'

They headed aft until they arrived at a large circular door of wine-dark wood. They looked at each other in confusion. There did not seem to be a handle but, after a few seconds' deliberation, Caelestis touched a metal disc at the centre. The door opened in sections, unfolding like a flower, and they stepped through into a cabin.

There was a bed draped with rich old tapestries and a table strewn with yellowing charts. A chair stood against the far bulkhead, beside a shelf full of curios.

And all the furniture had been made for someone at least two and a half metres tall.

'These must be Hunguk's quarters,' said Caelestis.

There was one other door directly opposite. Crossing to it, Altor listened and then opened it, sword at the ready. He stepped back in bewilderment. Instead of another cabin, he saw a haze of jumbled shapes and dizzying swirls.

Caelestis came up beside him. 'I can't seem to focus on it,' he said, staring intently into the vortex of drifting lines.

'Nor I. It's like . . . sometimes it seems a long tunnel, then just a flat . . .' Altor shook his head. 'Don't look at it, Caelestis.'

With difficulty Caelestis tore away his eyes. 'If the emeralds are in there, Susurrien can get them himself.'

'I'll search the table. You check out that shelf.'

Despite the need for haste, Altor could not resist a quick look at the charts. The fine calligraphy reminded him of the illuminated manuscripts at his monastery. That was as far as the resemblance went. These were like no charts or manuscripts he had ever seen before. Mythological places were mapped on a grid of ellipses and converging lines. Some of the symbols scrawled around the margin were in Arcane, a script Altor knew to be used by sorcerers. Others he could not identify.

The sound of Caelestis rummaging around on the shelves reminded Altor of the urgency of their work. He patted the manuscripts to check that nothing was hidden under them, then searched the table drawers.

Caelestis was giving each object only a moment's appraisal before tossing it over his shoulder. Some looked intriguing and he would have loved to know what they were for, but he forced himself to consider only the two emeralds for which Susurrien had sent them. A thief of some experience, he knew that there was sometimes a need for stealth and sometimes for speed.

A shrill vibration set their teeth on edge. It was coming from the vortex of light beyond the other door. They looked across to see it changing, the pattern of colours gradually settling to a steady grey-blue glare. In the midst of the light, a hulking shadow appeared and began to grow. Then they saw that it was not growing but coming nearer – a figure striding towards them along a tunnel that stretched to a far distant place.

'It's Hunguk,' gasped Caelestis. 'He's returned.'

NINE

THE PIRATE KING

Hunguk's silhouette grew until it filled the door frame, then he stepped from the swirling mass of light. Altor and Caelestis knew their time had run out.

Even in the tall cabin he had to stoop, and his shoulders were as broad as a rowboat's beam. In stature he resembled a rugged rock, strewn in kelp and clad in plates of iron that tolled like a bell as he raised his two huge axes. Eyes like molten silver sharpened over a dark, weather-beaten face.

When he spoke, they heard the voice of thunder. 'What mortal mice are these, come to scratch in my larder while I roam the world's waves? God's blood, I say, of all thieves the most reckless are those who presume to plunder Hunguk's hoard!' He clashed his axes together, sending sparks shooting in all directions. 'Come, you land-pests. Pit your weapons against the Lord of the Nine Seas – if you dare.'

Altor snatched up his sword, which he had laid close at hand while he searched the table. Caelestis reached to the empty scabbard at his belt, remembered he'd lost his sword escaping from the Roc, and instead pulled a dagger from his boot.

The two stood facing Hunguk. They were not eager for battle. It was easy to see that what Susurrien had told them was true: the Pirate King was no longer a mortal man. The long centuries had tempered him into a creature of myth. He was halfway to being a god of the seas.

Altor rushed in first. His sword clattered against the Pirate King's axe, slipped, glanced off thick armour-plate iron. The haft of the axe swung up, crashing into him with such force that all the wind was knocked out of his lungs. Altor slumped, his sword almost falling from nerveless fingers.

Caelestis saw the other axe raised for a death-blow. Disregarding the danger to himself, he leapt onto the table and from there jumped up to catch Hunguk's arm. It was like grappling with an oak tree. Kicking out blindly, Caelestis was rewarded by a snarl of annoyance as his foot landed in the Pirate King's mouth.

He let go of the arm, twisting in midair to land on his feet. 'Let's get out of here,' he yelled at Altor.

'We can't go without the emeralds.'

'I've got them.' Caelestis opened his palm to show two glittering green jewels that he had found in a clay jar just as Hunguk stepped out of the vortex.

Altor nodded. 'In that case, I'm right behind you!'

Hunguk roared as he swung up both axes to

strike. Altor waited a split second, pretending he was still stunned, only to fling himself out of the way as the attack came. The axes made a sound like two lethal catapault stones as they sliced through the air. Missing Altor by barely a hair's breadth, they chopped deep into the wood of the deck. Again Hunguk gave vent to his battle roar.

'Stand still!' he bellowed. 'I'll teach you to steal from the king of all reavers!'

Altor was not usually one to run from a battle, but he knew when he was overmatched. Seeing Caelestis disappear out of the cabin door, he dived after him just in time to evade a brutal kick from Hunguk's spiked boot.

They raced along the passage that led to the deck, with the Pirate King thundering in his fury behind them. His oaths shook the timbers of the ship like the rumbling of a storm, and they could hear the harsh clang of his armour as he strode heavily after them.

'Lucky he's not quick on his feet!' gasped Caelestis.

He hurled himself up the companionway and emerged into the chill air, only to duck instinctively as something whizzed past his head.

Altor came up beside him and, for an instant, both men paused in amazement. The scene had changed. The fog had been torn away by hard gusts of wind and strange geometric objects, like tangles of coloured thread, were flitting through the air all around them. Wherever these objects touched the hull or rigging, they exploded in a fountain of red sparks.

Worst of all, ahead of the ship loomed a jet-black void that looked like no place on earth.

They turned. The view to stern was like peering out of a vast round tunnel. The edges of reality itself twisted in a massive arc. They could see the island and the familiar ocean tinged by the afterglow of sunset, but they were receding with alarming speed.

The Devil's Runner was leaving the earthly plane!

Caelestis was first to get his bearings. 'To the horse – quick!' he cried.

But the horse had gone. They scanned the deck in horror as Hunguk's clanking footsteps thudded nearer.

'Look—'

Caelestis pointed to a shape moving beyond the rotted sails. For an instant they thought they glimpsed the horse hovering there, a laughing figure in dark robes riding on its back, but then a sheet of freezing drizzle swept down to obliterate their view.

With a splintering of wood Hunguk burst from the companionway, smashing the hatch aside in his eagerness to catch them. He stared about, gave a snarl as he sighted his prey, and came stamping towards them.

Altor and Caelestis spared a last glance forward. The well of blackness almost filled the sky. With the horse gone, there was nothing else for it. They ran to the rail and jumped overboard into the seething grey sea.

If Hunguk roared his fury at seeing them escape, they could not hear it over the surge of the waves. Swimming powerfully, they reached the island's shore and turned bedraggled to watch the departure of *The Devil's Runner*. It pulled a blanket of darkness behind it, like a low black reef against the horizon, and the ship was visible only as a blur in the heart of the darkness.

A wind seemed to catch the black cloud, even though the two heroes could feel no breeze, and sucked it away into the thin air. Only a few strands of mist were left, trailing across an empty sea that was swiftly becoming shrouded by nightfall.

The last waves from the strange ship's wake lapped at the shingle by their feet. When those were gone, the ocean all around lay still and silent under the canopy of awakening stars.

Altor and Caelestis looked at each other.

It was Altor who said what both had already realised: 'We're marooned.'

Caelestis watched the driftwood smoulder, glow, then catch alight. He blew until orange flames licked up, sending sparks spiralling into the night sky. Satisfied, he replaced the flint and tinder in his pocket and sat back to watch the stars.

Altor came up the beach. Caelestis heard the pebbles crunching under his feet before he saw him, outlined in the firelight against the black hump of the island's interior. In each hand he held a fish dangling on a line.

'Ever resourceful, eh?' said Caelestis, lying back and pillowing his head on his coat.

Altor squatted down, tossed a couple more pieces of driftwood on the fire, and took out his knife to prepare the fish. 'Why are you so cheerful?' he said. 'We're stranded here, we've no shelter, precious little to eat and no prospect of rescue. Normally you'd be the first to complain.'

Caelestis sighed. 'I can't explain it myself. But, after all, we did get the emeralds.'

Altor grunted. 'And a lot of good they'll do us, stuck here on this barren rock.'

'Something will turn up.' Caelestis took out his own knife and began idly to whittle at a bit of driftwood. 'Tomorrow we'll climb to the top of the island.'

Altor nodded. 'We'll have more chance of signalling a ship from there. Assuming any ships pass that close. Hey, what's this?'

His knife had struck something hard inside the fish's gut. He extracted it, cleaned it up, and held it to the firelight. The gold band shimmered like liquid, the dark jewel drank the light.

Caelestis glanced at it, blinked, and sat bolt upright. 'My ring!' He snatched it away and slipped it on his finger. 'It is, Altor! It's my ring.'

Altor whistled between his teeth. 'Surely it can't be a coincidence. You realise what this means, Cael? It's a sign of Divine Providence.

It means the Almighty Himself is watching over our quest.'

Caelestis' elation faded slightly as another explanation occurred to him. The Faltyn that inhabited the ring had once given a little of its life essence to raise Altor from the dead. It could mean the two were somehow linked, their destinies intertwined.

But Altor did not know this, and Caelestis doubted if he would appreciate learning of it now. What would it mean to a pious worshipper to know that part of his immortal soul had been fused with energy taken from a pagan sprite? Caelestis, who was scarcely more devout than a tomcat, cared little about such things himself, but he respected his friend's beliefs so he kept the secret to himself.

'The ring won't do us much good now,' he said. 'The Faltyn couldn't conjure up a ship for us – and even if it could, we've nothing to pay it with.'

'That doesn't matter.' Altor went back to filleting the fish with considerably bolstered spirits. 'I know now that you were right. Something will turn up.'

They had rarely had a more strenuous day, and it was all they could do to stay awake while the fish cooked. Caelestis wolfed down his portion and then stretched out beside the fire. The hard-packed sand made an uncomfortable mattress, but for once he was too weary to care. By the time Altor had returned from the water's edge, where he had gone to clean his knife, Caelestis was sound asleep.

He was woken by a metallic clanking that sounded like a cowbell. Opening his eyes, he saw that the sky was that pale jade colour that comes before the dawn.

He turned over and groaned. The way he'd been lying in the night had made his back stiff, and now that he was more alert he realised how hungry he was. 'I think we should make every effort to get off this island as soon as possible,' he said to Altor.

There was no reply. Sitting up, Caelestis noticed his friend kneeling in prayer some way off down the beach. As was his habit, he had obviously risen early to meditate and practise his swordplay. Caelestis glowered at the rock pools further down the beach. Either he would have to wait for his breakfast, or he'd have to see about catching something himself.

A wave rolled in and another hollow clang reminded Caelestis of the sound that had intruded on his dreams. He looked round and saw a flask of yellow copper bobbing up and down against a washed-up clump of seaweed.

Caelestis glanced back at Altor, thought for a moment, then got up and made his way down to the water. He stared down at the flask, which was sealed with a lead bung that caused it to float upside down. After a few seconds' deliberation he shrugged and picked it up. A curious glyph was stamped into the bung, but Caelestis had no idea what it meant.

'It might contain a message,' he said to

himself. 'Or better still, maybe it's a bottle of good brandy.'

And, with a little effort, he pulled out the bung.

The first Altor knew that anything was amiss was when his prayers were interupted by a sound like wind howling up a drainpipe. He muttered a quick 'Amen', crossed himself, and looked down to the water's edge.

Caelestis was standing beside a thick column of black smoke.

Then in the space of a blink it had changed. It was no longer smoke. Now it was a giant leg.

Altor didn't waste time thinking. He grabbed his sword and set off down the beach at a run.

Caelestis had fallen to one knee in simple shock. As Altor came running up, he looked from him to the giant figure that now stood astride the shore. 'What is it?' he gasped.

Altor saw the open copper bottle lying in the sand at his feet and guessed at once. 'A jinni.'

They craned their necks to look up at the giant. His head appeared to scrape the clouds, while his legs, knotted with individual cords of muscle each as thick as a tree, were planted solidly on the sand. As they watched he lifted his face exultantly and stretched both arms wide, giving a groan of satisfaction at being free that sounded like a fissure cracking open in a mountainside. He was clothed in nothing but the long dusty strands of his unkempt hair and beard, which reached right down to his knees like ivy covering a fortress wall.

'He's bigger than Skrymir . . .' said Altor. Now that he had time to take stock of the jinni, he felt rather foolish for brandishing a sword at him. His best lunge could barely have reached the jinni's ankle.

But Caelestis had recovered from his initial stupefaction. 'A jinni, eh?' he said, getting up and brushing the sand off his trousers. 'That's rather handy.'

Like a man noticing a gnat, the jinni became

aware of them. He stooped, his mouth opening to reveal snaggled black teeth, and a gust of foul breath almost knocked them down. Above that cavernous maw, huge eyes burned like torches.

'Where and when, how and why?' he boomed. 'Tell me your tale, you who have freed me.'

Before Altor could say anything, Caelestis was shaking his head. 'We've no time for pleasantries,' he called up to the jinni. 'We ought to be in Hakbad. So, your first task is to create a winged chariot—'

The jinni gave a shout of laughter that almost deafened them. 'My first *task*? You've got things muddled, little man. There'll be no wishes, no orders. Pleas for mercy would be more like it, but even they'd be wasted. In a moment I'll lift my foot, and the sight of it descending is the last thing you'll see.'

'What?' Caelestis blinked in dismay and pointed to the copper flask. 'But . . . but I freed you. You've got to give me three wishes.' He looked at the jinni's face and went pale. 'Haven't you?'

'Don't remind me of that flask!' roared the jinni angrily. 'After a wizard tricked me into it, I waited for a hundred years and not a day went by but I promised I'd bestow lavish riches on whoever let me out. But did you free me then? So, for the next two hundred years, I swore each day that whoever freed me would receive all the treasures and honours of the world. But did you free me *then*? As the next four hundred years passed, I pledged that the one who opened the flask would be rewarded with the three wishes of his heart, wealth and power that no mortal has ever dreamed of, a kingdom where his word was the only law, and eternal youth so that he could enjoy these things to the end of time . . .'

The jinni paused, bending over the beach so that his face blotted out the sky. 'But did you free me THEN? No! This is why you now find me in a quite different frame of mind. After seven hundred years, I decided that the penalty for leaving me trapped so long in the flask would be instant death. And so, little man, prepare to die.'

The jinni lifted his foot and held it poised like a slab of mountainside, ready to crush the life out of Caelestis and Altor. Then it started to descend.

TEN

The Prisoner of the Cyclops

'Coward!' Altor shouted up at the jinni. The foot hovered uncertainly just a metre overhead, then slowly moved aside to give them a glimpse of those two blazing eyes under a frowning brow like a shelf of black granite. 'Oh? What did you say?'

The jinni's expression was one of surprise, gradually giving way to rage. Caelestis turned to his friend and spoke behind his hand. 'You've got a plan?'

Altor shook his head. He had no idea what

he was doing. But, although he was aware of the absurdity of challenging a creature as huge as the jinni, he knew he had to try something.

He held up his sword in a defiant gesture. 'I have fought all manner of creatures, foul and fell, that the Devil has put upon this earth. Do you fear to face me in battle?'

The jinni folded his arms across his massive chest and shook with laughter. 'What do you suggest? What kind of contest could be fair?' He grinned, displaying teeth like ancient crags. 'As you see, I am unarmed!'

Altor ignored the sarcasm. A plan was beginning to suggest itself. It was a long shot, certainly, but better than being crushed like a bug.

'We'll wrestle,' he said. 'The first of us to fall is the loser, and must submit to the victor's will.'

The jinni could not contain his merriment. Tears of laughter swept the dust from his cheeks. 'You are mad. I'll knock you off your feet with one clap.'

The jinni drew his hands up in front of him. The muscles of his forearms swelled like boulders. The palms alone were bigger than cathedral doors, each finger-joint the size of a church pew. Altor did not doubt that when they came together the shock wave would send both him and Caelestis flying.

He stepped smartly forward and drove his sword-blade under the jinni's toenail, right up to the hilt.

It seemed to take the pain a second or two to reach the jinni's brain. He froze with a startled look on his face, hands braced a few dozen metres apart. Then he let out a long screech that made the island shudder. Clutching his injured foot, he hopped backwards, issuing a torrent of threats, curses and cries of pain.

His other heel landed on a boulder, half buried in the wet sand, that the low tide had uncovered. The surface had been worn smooth by centuries of pounding by waves and was slimy with kelp.

As the jinni's good foot slipped out from under him, the look on his face changed. Rage and pain evaporated into simple dismay. Arms flailing comically, he swayed, lost his balance, and fell over backwards.

Caelestis and Altor hit the ground just in time. As the jinni landed in the shallows there was a splash like a tidal wave. Water cascaded down for what felt like an eternity, soaking the two heroes to the skin.

They got to their feet to see the jinni lying stretched out from the shore. The look on his face was no longer so fierce – more puzzled and full of chagrin. Altor could almost feel sorry for him, but he had to follow up his advantage. He strode over to the jinni's foot, reached up, and retrieved his sword.

'Had enough?'

As much through shame as honour, the jinni was forced to admit defeat. Hauling himself up, he knelt in the surf and wrung the salt water out of his beard.

'Master,' he said, 'I am yours to command. Tell me the three wishes of your heart and I shall grant them.'

Altor and Caelestis looked at each other. 'That's better, isn't it?'

'A great improvement,' admitted Caelestis. 'For the first wish, tell him to take us to Hakbad.'

Altor had not had time to think of the danger while he was acting, but now he discovered he was shaking – through shock rather than fear, but Altor was a proud young man and did not want to let on. Speaking loudly so that his voice didn't betray it, he commanded the jinni to transport them to Hakbad.

The jinni placed his hand in front of them on the sand, palm up. 'Hakbad, the City of Stars,' he said, as they climbed up. 'It was well-known even before my imprisonment in that accursed bottle. I shall enjoy the chance to see it again – those majestic spires and patterned domes, the terraced palace gardens, the tree-lined avenues . . .'

Lifting the two friends, he turned and began to wade through the sea.

'Ouch, this is uncomfortable,' said Caelestis, as he tried to find a way to sit on the hard callouses of the jinni's hand. 'I wish I had a cushion!'

'Here you are, young master,' said the jinni, producing from nowhere a black silk cushion with golden tassels.

Altor was furious. 'That doesn't count! He was just thinking aloud.'

Possibly the jinni smiled in the grey depths of his beard. 'Pardon me, master, but it must always be exactly three wishes. That is the way of these things, and it's not for you or me to say otherwise. If you do not wish to waste the wish that still remains, you must refrain from thinking aloud.'

Altor fumed to hear this, but Caelestis took it in his stride. Settling himself on the cushion, he said, 'No matter. We can use the last wish to find the Sword of Life. We won't need the jinni after that.'

The shallow waters at the head of the Gulf of Marazid were no higher to the jinni than a stream to a mortal man. He strode on through water that came to his waist, and as he went storm clouds gathered. They churned around him and swept out behind from his shoulders like a cloak until the sun was blotted out and the sky turned a violent grey-black. Talons of lightning shuddered across the heavens. Without being asked, the jinni cupped his hands to shelter them from the rain.

'He's not totally intractable, you see?' said Caelestis, peering out at the storm between the cracks in the jinni's fingers.

Altor was still smarting over the wasted wish. 'I hope that cushion's comfortable,' was all he would say.

The day wore on and all they could hear were the gusting wind and the heavy sloshing sound as the jinni made his ponderous way eastwards into the Sea of Lament.

Suddenly Caelestis stared intently out into the rain. 'There's a light!' he said. 'Jinni, wait.'

'Be careful what you say!' cried Altor, in alarm. 'Don't use the word "wish", whatever you do.'

The jinni opened his cupped hands, exposing the two to the rain. 'Did you call, masters?' he asked.

Caelestis pointed to the light. It winked atop a narrow spire of rock that jutted vertically up from the sea. The peak was roughly on a level with the jinni's head. 'What's that place?'

'It is the tower of Saknathur the wizard, little master. Best we don't go too close. Saknathur does not care for visitors.'

Caelestis shook his head. 'Look again.'

The jinni squinted through the heavy curtain of rain. The tower was a pile of rubble and the buildings at its base mere weathered shells, clinging to the peak like barnacles.

'Hunguk the Pirate King slew Saknathur forty decades ago,' said Altor.

'Ah.' The jinni looked wistful. 'Even Saknathur is gone, eh? I was imprisoned so long.'

Caelestis turned to his friend. 'Saknathur's fortress is legendary. In the ruins we'd be bound to find a dozen magic trinkets.'

'I don't think this is the time to think of money.'

'I don't mean we'd sell them.' Caelestis held up his ring. 'We can use them to pay the Faltyn. It likes magic stuff. Maybe it'll even help us find the Sword of Life, so we could cut out Susurrien *and* save our last wish from the jinni.'

'Well . . . maybe. I wouldn't mind a chance to stretch my legs, anyway. Jinni!'

'Yes, tiny master?'

'How would you like to stop here for a breather?'

The jinni squinted at them. 'This is not a wish, then?'

'It's not a wish, but we would like to spend a little time here before continuing on to Hakbad.' This time Altor was obstinate, and when the jinni didn't reply at once he gave a casual wave. 'Oh, well, it's of no great importance. Wade on, then, if you must.'

'Be not so hasty,' said the jinni. 'I merely wanted to clarify how things stood. For a fact, an hour's rest would be much appreciated. Seven centuries in that bottle has left my knees quite stiff.'

He waded over to the ruined fortress and lifted up his hand to a marble balustrade. Caelestis and Altor stepped across onto a parapet that ran right round the remains of the central tower.

The light they had seen came from the colonnade at the back of the parapet. Caelestis led the way, then paused and looked back at the jinni, who was leaning with his elbow on a lichen-spotted crag. 'You'll wait here for us, then.'

The jinni shrugged. 'I'm too big to come

inside with you. I'll wait till . . . midnight, let's say.'

All three looked up at the sky, which boiled black with storm clouds. At a guess it was now late afternoon, but in fact it could have been any hour of the day or night. 'Let's say three hours from now,' decided Altor.

The jinni nodded. 'Agreed.'

Altor and Caelestis hurried out of the rain, stepping through an archway off the colonnade that led into a large hall.

At just that moment, the storm outside abated and the clouds parted so that a shaft of blood-coloured light from the setting sun shot through a high window at the far end of the room. It mingled with the light of a fire, and in that lurid glow they beheld a strange sight.

A giant woman, as tall as a palm tree and with coal-black skin, sat beside the fire. She had a large iron pot between her knees and with her bare hands she was scooping from it gobbets of greasy stew.

Altor and Caelestis instinctively ducked out

of sight behind a pile of rubble. They were just in time. A moment later the giantess turned to look in their direction, and from their hiding-place they saw that she had only a single eye – a yellow-green orb that rolled in its socket in the centre of her brow.

'A Cyclops!' whispered Altor.

They scanned the rest of the room. Just behind the Cyclops was an iron cage that at first they had not noticed. Its lone occupant came forward into the firelight: an old man with a long beard. He was dressed in tunic and leggings of grey cotton and had an overrobe of scuffed blue velvet. He looked as if he had seen better days. Gripping the bars of the cage, he watched the Cyclops as she consumed her meal.

'Did he see us?' said Caelestis, under his breath.

It seemed as if the old man looked a long time in their direction, then he turned to the Cyclops and gave a hiss of disgust.

She turned her head, putting up a shovel-sized hand to shield her eye from the sunset. 'What is it?' they heard her say scornfully. 'Would you like to share my supper?'

The old man wrung his hands. 'Ah, you fiend! I pray it clogs in your entrails and causes you unendurable pain.'

The Cyclops scowled to hear this, then gave an unpleasant bark of laughter. 'On the contrary, all of your companions have provided me with very appetising meals.' She tossed aside the empty pot; it clanged against the wall. 'Now I think I'll take a little nap. When I wake it'll be your turn.'

She rose and went to sling a few pieces of wood onto the fire. To Altor and Caelestis they looked like the broken timbers of a ship. For a poker she used a rusted old anchor, prodding the embers until the wood caught alight.

'Hmm,' said Caelestis, 'let me try something.'

He stepped out of hiding while the Cyclops'

back was turned and lobbed the cushion that the jinni had given him. It landed just behind her. As she looked round, Caelestis drew back out of sight.

'Did you hear anything?' the Cyclops asked the old man in the cage.

'Nothing. Perhaps what you heard was the heavy tread of your own guilt, you thing of perfect evil.'

'Bah,' she said, forgetting the noise. 'How can a creature of perfect evil know guilt?' As she stepped back from the fire, her heel brushed the cushion. 'Why, what's this? A pillow . . . how delightful. And it matches my complexion! Strange I never noticed it before but, no matter, at last I have a pillow on which to rest my dainty head.'

A fallen masonry slab served her as a couch. As she was about to lie down, the old man called to her. 'Wait. If I'm to be eaten when you wake, at least grant me a final wish.'

'No!' The Cyclops rocked with mirth.

'Listen, I beg you. Grant me this wish or my bitterness will spoil your meal.'

The Cyclops considered this. 'Very well,' she said at last. 'What is the wish?'

He pointed to a pile of rucksacks beside the fire. 'Among my companions' belongings there is a lyre. Let me play a last tune to mourn their passing.'

'And spoil my nap? Fie!'

'Why is your anger so impatient? The elegy is beautiful and haunting. Its soft notes will lull you to sleep. You'll waken with improved appetite.'

'Agh! Words, words, words! You and your fellows scatter words like – I know not what! Every time you open your mouth it is as though a swarm of bees pours out to vex me. If you weren't the last, and your tongue the next succulent morsel I shall taste, I would ask God to give me one ear to match my one eye.'

'You use ten words to my one,' said the old man quietly. 'Now, am I to get my lyre or not?'

'Yes, all right. Just let me sleep, curse you.' She ripped open the bags and, finding the lyre, handed it to him peevishly.

As the Cyclops stretched out, carefully positioning the cushion under her huge head, the old man began to play a wistful song. The notes were quiet, the melody seductive. Immersed for a short time in the serene beauty of the song, Altor and Caelestis were surprised when they heard the Cyclops' snores rasping like a saw cutting down a tree.

They peeped out from their hiding-place. 'It's all right, she's asleep,' hissed the old man.

They strode softly down the hall and opened the cage. Altor kept a wary eye on the sleeping Cyclops. 'I never thought such creatures existed,' he said.

The old man was almost weeping with relief at his rescue. 'They do – the worst luck for me and my twenty-three companions. She ate every one, and later tonight she planned to eat me.'

'We should keep our voices down,' said Altor.

The old man shook his head. 'No, no, she won't wake in a hurry. That song I sang was a powerful enchantment I learned from a bard in Cornumbria.'

The Cyclops indeed appeared sound asleep. 'Really?' said Caelestis, privately thinking it was the jinni's pillow that had done the trick.

As they walked back along the hall, away from where the Cyclops lay, Altor asked the old man how he had come to be imprisoned.

'The story is long, but I will be brief,' said the old man. 'Set among the Drakken foothills in the north of Kurland lies the Monastery of the Reawakening. My companions, who were all eaten by that pitiless creature, were the senior monks. I was their abbot. Our mission was one of great import to all mankind, and we had spent years preparing for it. As you may be aware, the dawn of the new millennium is only a few years away. It will be the time for Our Lord to set aside

His work – this earth – and begin anew. Evil will be pulled from the world like a weed. The Devil and his followers will be for ever expunged. Our descendants will find the coming millennium to be the era of God's kingdom on earth . . .'

Altor and Caelestis nodded gravely, saying nothing. They had heard another myth that the year 1000 would be Doomsday, a time of storms and plagues and bloody wars. It was then that the gates of Spyte would open and the Five Magi return from the night skies to rule the world. Unless they could stop them.

'This heaven-on-earth will not come about without a struggle,' added the abbot, as if reading their thoughts. 'Many imagine heaven to be their birthright, but in fact God will judge man's worthiness by the vigour with which we are prepared to fight for it. He can provide guidance, but it falls to mortal men to destroy the evil that has plagued us since the world began. If we canot do that for ourselves, we forfeit Paradise.'

He seemed to be ranting, perhaps near to hysteria after his long ordeal, and Altor put a hand on his shoulder to calm him. 'Peace, my lord abbot . . .'

'No, listen to me,' insisted the abbot, with vehemence. 'There is something you must do. You see, we travelled so far from our monastery to recover something that will be needed on the final day: a sapling ash, nurtured through many generations by the monks of our order. It was grown from a key taken from Yggdrasil, the Tree of Life, which was the first tree in the Garden of Eden.'

Altor frowned, not liking to hear what was coming. 'And how can we help?'

'The sapling was stolen from us by a sect of Opalarian fire worshippers serving the god Tammuz. They used witchery to penetrate our wards, then flew off with the sapling on a bridge of flame. Now all my colleagues are dead, so there is no one but you I can turn to. The sapling must be recovered, I implore you, as it is to stand for the new era just as Yggdrasil stood for the one that is past.'

'So what do you want us to do?' said Caelestis.

The abbot fixed him with a look of passionate conviction. 'I want you to go to Opalar and take it back!'

ELEVEN

The Fire Worshippers

'What do you think?'

Caelestis glanced back along the hall to where the abbot was rummaging among his belongings. 'I can't see how we can help him.'

Altor sighed. 'But his quest is a good one, he has sore need of our aid. How can we refuse?'

'We'll explain that we're already on a quest. If we don't get the Sword of Life and stop the Magi, the new millennium will never dawn.'

The abbot came back clutching a haversack stuffed with books. 'I'm ready to set out. How did you arrive here?'

'It'll be easier if we just show you,' said

Caelestis. He led the abbot through to the parapet where the jinni was lounging against the cliff.

The abbot gave a gasp. 'A Ta'ashim demon! Get back before it sees us!'

'Ah, there you are,' said the jinni, ignoring him. 'And who's this old chap? He seems rather excitable.'

'Show some respect,' said Altor sternly. 'He's an abbot.'

The abbot looked from one to the other. 'You . . . you *know* this creature? You control it?'

'It's a long story,' said Caelestis.

The jinni stretched out his hand to the balustrade. 'Ready to go on to Hakbad now?' he said. 'Say farewell to your friend the abbot and we'll be on our way.'

'Are you familiar with the sect of the god Tammuz in Opalar?' Altor asked the jinni, rather to Caelestis' annoyance.

'You want to go to *Opalar* now? Make up your mind!'

'If we were to go to Hakbad via Opalar—'

'That would be two wishes,' said the jinni. 'You'd have none left.'

'No,' said the abbot. 'The sapling has to be brought back here, to Saknathur's fortress. There's an astral gateway that leads back from here to the monastery.'

'I'll take you to Opalar and back,' offered the jinni, 'but that's the best I can do. I shouldn't allow you to go back on the wish to travel to Hakbad, but we've hardly started on that one yet.'

Caelestis turned to the abbot. 'So, for your convenience, we should end up stranded here,' he said in an accusatory tone.

Altor put a hand on his friend's arm. 'Peace, Caelestis. It's the only sure and safe route for getting the sapling back to its rightful home. We'll find a way to get to Hakbad from here, I'm sure of it.'

Caelestis flung up his hands. 'I cannot argue with you! Come along, then, let's get on with it.'

'Excellent!' Clapping his hands delightedly, the abbot went to mount the balustrade.

'Better you stay here,' said Altor. 'With all due respect, adventuring is no sort of activity for a venerable gentleman like yourself.'

Both knew that to take the abbot would jeopardise their chance of success. But he was reluctant to stay behind, and it took some argument before they finally persuaded him.

'What about the Cyclops?' said Altor, as he and Caelestis clambered back onto the jinni's hand.

The abbot drew a shortsword from his rucksack and smiled grimly. 'I know how to deal with ungodly creatures like that, my son. I haven't always been a doddering old man.'

Altor nodded. 'Be careful.'

'And you. God watch over you both.'

He had to shout the last words as the jinni swept them away from the parapet and began the journey east on long, swift strides. Looking back, they saw the abbot haloed by flickering firelight from the hall. Bowed as he was in prayer, it made him look like a saint depicted on a church window.

They watched until Saknathur's palace was a sliver of dark against the grey sky, all sign of the abbot and the firelight now lost in the gathering night.

'I've just noticed something,' said Caelestis. 'We're flying.'

It was true. The jinni had risen out of the sea and was climbing steadily into the sky.

Thunder muttered below the horizon. The wind drove a last gust of cool rain, then they were through the clouds and surrounded by a blaze of silver starlight.

Caelestis looked down between the cracks in the jinni's fingers. A sea of clouds swept by below. It looked like smoke frozen in time.

'What would they see, those who looked up now?' he mused aloud.

The jinni gave a loud peal of laughter. 'Honest Ta'ashim who glance out into the night may catch a glimpse of us in the sudden flash of a lightning stroke. They will think they see a demon out of their folk-tales.' His laughter subsided as he fixed a smouldering gaze on the east, and when he spoke again it was with hatred in his voice: 'But as for any Tammuz cultists who should chance to look westwards . . . I encountered their sect in ancient times, and it was one of them who sealed me in the flask. They would see an avenging angel!'

Roused by the warmth of dawn, Altor and Caelestis took stock of their surroundings and remembered they were in the jinni's hand. They looked down. Jagged mountain peaks, misted by soft cloud, shimmered in the pink sunrise.

'The Harogarn Mountains,' said Altor. 'We're close to our destination.'

The jinni noticed they were awake. 'I have been brooding on the priesthood of Tammuz,' he said dourly, eyes smouldering at a heartfelt grudge. 'It seems unjust that the old ways should all have passed while I was trapped – Saknathur dead, the old lands of Kaikuhuru sundered – and yet that pernicious cult endures.'

'You said it was they who imprisoned you?' asked Altor.

The jinni made a rumbling sound deep in his chest as he thought back. 'The priests of Tammuz venerate fire as a vampire sect venerates blood. We jinn were created from fire, and if they capture one of us they try to draw out his fire, reducing him to a lifeless husk. If they cannot do that they quench his fire and force him into servitude. With me they could do neither.'

'I would think you'd welcome the chance to be revenged on them, then,' said Caelestis, 'rather than charging us one of our three wishes for this journey.'

'Revenge? Yes!' declared the jinni. 'In my breast I feel the old passions of my race. The flames of retribution are stoked. When we confront the Tammuz cult, I will pit my might alongside your own!'

With an even grimmer cast to his jaw, the jinni began to descend towards the mountaintops. Altor turned to Caelestis with a worried look. 'So much for the subtle approach,' he said quietly.

'A diversion could be just what we need,' countered Caelestis. 'While you and the jinni keep the cultists busy, I'll sneak in and find the sapling.' He saw the dubious look on his friend's face. 'Trust me, thievery is one thing I know all about.'

The stronghold of the Tammuz cult had appeared on the horizon. It looked almost as if it had been chipped from the cliffs where it sat. Dawn light glanced off the minarets, sharp cornices and faceted columns of glassy grey–black stone. The sunrise behind it made it seem as if the walls were afire.

The central tower rose above an egg-shaped dome encrusted with carnelian and topaz. Among the grey buildings the dome glimmered like a second sun, catching and magnifying the rays of the dawn until they became painful to look upon. Onto the terrace in front swarmed figures in robes of gold and scarlet, and as the stronghold sped closer the babble of excited voices rose in the chill morning air.

Caelestis pointed to the central tower. 'Put me down there and then you can launch your attack.'

The jinni circled the tower, reaching out so that Caelestis could leap across to its balcony. 'Good luck,' called Altor.

'Luck?' said Caelestis. 'I make my own.'

Caelestis was as casual as if he were about to play hopscotch. Bracing himself, he jumped across from the jinni's fingertip and sailed breathtakingly down towards the balcony. Just an instant before he landed, their circuit of the tower took Altor and the jinni around the side of the dome so that they lost sight of him.

The cultists were milling about on the terrace below. As the jinni descended, the adepts of the sect came pouring out from the dome. They were resplendent in gold breastplates and high copper crowns, and in their midst stood a figure Altor took to be the high priest. With curt gestures he marshalled his adepts into position around him.

The jinni swept lower. Now Altor could see the look on the high priest's face.

He was smiling.

The adepts began to chant: a single high, clear note. Magical force fairly crackled in the air. The high priest raised aloft his wand – a fabulous thing of gold and shimmering jewels, it caught a shaft of sunlight—

And *threw* it at them.

Altor just had time to close his eyes, then it was as if his eyelids had become transparent and he was staring into the heart of the sun. Blistering heat surrounded them, and a flare of light like the birth of the world.

Gasping in pain, the jinni closed his hand. Altor had to strain his muscles to keep from being crushed, but in fact the jinni's reflex had saved him from being burned to death. For a moment he passed out; then, as awareness returned, he realised they were falling—

'Jinni!'

The jinni gave a groan. 'I'm not finished yet.'

Pulling out of the dive, he planted his massive feet on the crags of rock below the stronghold and stooped, staring fiercely down at the terrace like a man peering into an anthill.

It was a ploy calculated to overawe the adepts. It worked; several quailed, faltering in their chant. The high priest snapped a rebuke as he levelled his wand for another blast.

It was a long jump down to the terrace but Altor did it without thinking. Anything was better than even a glancing hit from the wand's fireburst. As he landed the silver sword was already in his hand. Raising it high, he rushed towards the circle of adepts. Now he could see that a network of flickering energy flowed between them and their high priest. And there was something else: as the nearest adept flinched away from Altor's charge, the nimbus of light dimmed slightly.

Altor guessed that breaking the chant was the key to victory. But before he could reach the circle of adepts, armoured guards wielding dumbbell-shaped bronze maces ran forward from the dome to cut him off. He had never faced as many foes. Desperately he swung his sword as, above his head, the jinni and the high priest traded bolts of coruscating flame.

'Hurry, Caelestis,' muttered Altor to himself. 'We can't hold this lot off for long.'

Inside the tower, Caelestis had not been idling. Taking the steps half a dozen at a time he reached the bottom of the staircase. He dived through a high archway and found himself inside the dome. In the centre was a low altar stone of red granite on which rested a large crystalline egg. Sunlight filtered in through the topaz inlays of the dome, forming a rich pink glow in which the egg seemed to pulse with inner life.

Caelestis stepped forward, hesitated, picked

it up. The hard crystal surface tingled under his touch.

A noise like an earthquake resounded dully through the dome. It was the jinni's roar of pain and fury. Reminded of the need for haste, Caelestis looked around and saw a spiral stairway leading to the lower floor of the dome. The egg tucked under one arm, he hurried down.

Below was a pillared shrine festooned with copper decorations, but Caelestis took in all the details at a glance. Outside he could see the terrace where the high priest and his adepts were locked in battle against the jinni. Spells of fire and black smoke thickened the air. The sustained high-pitched note of the adepts' chant throbbed like the singing of distant stars.

The high priest gestured, causing a pall of grey mist to close around the jinni's throat. The jinni staggered and seemed about to fall, but then he used his own magic to summon a thunderous gale that broke apart the mist.

The clash of weapons drew Caelestis' attention to a corner of the terrace where Altor was struggling with a group of warrior-priests. One swung his mace, Altor ducked, and the blow struck stone chips out of the balustrade behind him.

Caelestis remembered what he had come for. The sapling. He scanned the room, but it was nowhere in sight.

There was a fiery hiss, and blinding golden light flooded in from outside. Caelestis squinted towards the battle, where he saw the high priest stab a bolt of white-hot energy into the jinni's flesh. The jinni gave a great howl of agony as he writhed, caught by the devastating power of the wand. He began to shrivel under the onslaught.

Then Caelestis noticed the egg. It was pulsing even more violently now. The vibration that emanated from it was matched by the eerie chanting of the adepts, and it gave an unmistakable flicker of light every time the high priest called on the power of his wand.

Caelestis looked into the crystalline depths. Something moved sinuously there, like a golden serpent waiting to hatch.

'Oh, hang it,' said Caelestis. 'There's nothing else I can try.' And he flung the egg down onto the hard marble floor.

On the terrace outside, Altor heard a roar of flame. He looked past the guard he was fighting to see long tongues of fire shoot out from the dome. One engulfed a group of adepts, who fell screaming with their robes ablaze. Another scattered the guards. Altor took advantage of the distraction to smash his opponent's clumsy weapon aside and punch him to the ground with the hilt of his sword.

The glow faded from the high priest's wand and he stared at it in confusion and fear. The jinni, reeling from the punishing attack that had almost slain him, saw his chance. He threw up his hands and brought them together with titanic force. A thunderflash sizzled down towards the high priest, who tried in vain to deflect it with his wand.

The next moment he was blotted out by a fireball. The accompanying rush of wind knocked Altor off his feet. Lying prone, he felt his eyebrows singe from the furnace-like wave of heat.

It passed. There was silence. Altor looked up and grimaced in horror. All that remained of the high priest was a blackened skeleton clutching a golden wand. Before his eyes the skeleton took one step, swayed, and fell apart like a bundle of twigs.

He looked around. Some adepts were still on their feet, but the fight had gone out of them. They watched wide-eyed as the jinni scooped up the guards Altor had been fighting and flung them mercilessly into the chasm. Their screams echoed off the mountains, fading into stillness.

Altor felt dazed. 'What happened?' he said. 'I thought we were done for.'

The jinni nodded. 'The high priest's power was greater than mine. He would have won, but something stripped it away.'

Altor looked towards the dome. 'Caelestis . . .'

He gradually became aware of a pit of dread in his heart. He headed towards the dome, breaking into a run as he spotted a figure lying in the middle of a soot-blackened patch of marble floor where shards of a broken crystal egg sparkled dimly.

Altor skidded to a halt when he was still six metres from the fallen figure. That was close enough to see that nothing could be done for him. He had taken the brunt of the fireball that had been released when the egg shattered.

It was only by the ring on the corpse's finger that Altor could tell it was Caelestis.

TWELVE

The City of Stars

'This is what you wanted. The sapling from the Tree of Life.'

Altor turned. He had been staring blindly down into the mountain passes, lost in his brooding thoughts. He looked with dull eyes at the surviving cultists who had gathered nervously on the terrace.

The jinni stood astride two mountains, arms folded across his massive chest. 'Don't trust them. It could be a fake.'

The foremost of the cultists, face raw from burns sustained in the battle, held up the sapling. A halo of light hung around the grey branches – perhaps just the glow of the dawn, perhaps something more.

'It's no fake,' said Altor bleakly. He reached out and took the sapling. Success had never been so bitter.

Fearing the anger they sensed simmering inside him, the Tammuz cultists slunk away. Altor gazed for a long time at the sapling in his hand without speaking a word. At last he heaved a sigh. 'We should return. The abbot will be waiting.'

'Be of good cheer,' said the jinni. 'To win such a victory with only one casualty is lucky indeed.'

'I cannot agree,' said Altor, 'since it was my best friend who died. And for what? A shrub with but a single leaf.'

'Do you imagine that great magic must always come in the shape of a sword, or wand, or ring of precious metal?' The jinni gave a snort of contempt. 'Man, what you hold in your hand is the root of the life that is to come. As lost Eden was a place of verdure and plenty, so that sapling will grow to nourish the world of the next millennium.'

Altor shrugged. He was about to climb back onto the jinni's hand when a thought struck him like a hammer-blow between the eyes. He stood blinking, then looked slowly from the sapling to the wrapped body of his friend, which lay in the jinni's palm.

'How does it work?' he said.

The jinni was at first puzzled, then a deep frown creased his brow as it dawned on him what Altor was thinking. 'You cannot use it in that way,' he warned. 'Its magic is intended for a higher purpose.'

Altor jumped up onto the hand and with trembling fingers unwrapped the body. The dead black featureless face that was revealed was unrecognisable as Caelestis, so full of life and charm.

'Did you hear?' said the jinni, more urgently. 'It is not meant—'

Altor lifted the sapling. Its single leaf shone as green as all the fields of Ellesland.

Thunder muttered in the distance beyond the mountains. If it was a warning, Altor ignored it. Before the jinni could speak again, he had torn off the leaf and placed it in the corpse's mouth.

A lightning flash sizzled across an otherwise clear sky. Altor fell back stunned, feeling that it had barely missed him.

A heady smell rose around him. Ozone and salt spray, rich loam and ripe corn. The air sparked and tingled.

The jinni gave a gasp and lifted his hand to peer in amazement. From where he lay sprawled against the jinni's thumb, Altor looked across at Caelestis' body. It was wreathed in silver mist that steamed rapidly away like dew in the sunrise.

He heard a groan and reached for the shroud just as Caelestis sat upright – unmarked, his flesh as smooth and pink as if he had just got out of a bath.

'What happened to my clothes?' was the first thing he said.

They arrived back at Saknathur's tower still arguing.

'I don't believe it,' said Caelestis, shaking his head. 'I obviously wasn't that badly hurt, that's all.'

'Hurt?' cried Altor, eyes popping in exasperation. 'You were *dead*!'

'Burnt to the proverbial crisp,' put in the jinni, nodding.

The abbot was standing on the parapet to meet them. As soon as he saw the sapling, he folded his hands together and shut his eyes in a brief prayer.

'Am I dreaming?' he said, as they stepped down from the jinni's hand. 'Has the Devil sent a vision of vain hope to torment me in my sleep? No, I can feel the green wood, smell the scent of the sap . . . The final assurance is to pinch myself. Ow! Neither wine nor honey-cake could be as delicious as the pain of that pinch, for it tells me I am awake and the sapling is back in safe hands.'

'Think nothing of it,' said Caelestis, loftily.

He had wrapped one of the fire cultists' robes around him like a toga, giving himself the appearance of a rakish young patrician of the Old Selentine Empire. 'This sort of thing's all in a day's work for us,' he added, still refusing to accept that there had been the slightest hitch in their mission, much less that he himself had been fatally injured.

Altor decided that further argument was worthless. 'Whatever may be so, the whole venture will come to naught if we don't recover the blade we seek. Without that, the Magi will return to earth and there will be no Second Millennium.'

'You mentioned an astral gateway,' said Caelestis, to the abbot. 'Could we use it to reach Hakbad?'

The abbot shook his head woefully. 'It was created by Brother Pereus, who had been a wizard before he turned to the True Faith. But the Cyclops ate him, God shrivel her soul in torment, and I know how to use it only to return to the monastery. Now I must bid you farewell. I pray you will be delivered safely to Hakbad somehow.'

He shook hands with them and, with the sapling in his hands, went over to a section of wall where they could just make out a shimmering in the air. 'Lord, excuse me this witchery,' he said. 'I employ it only to do good in your name. So then: *vestigia nulla retrorsum*.'

With those words, he stepped into nowhere.

Altor and Caelestis fought the urge to rub their eyes. 'That's a handy little trick,' said Caelestis after a moment. 'If only we had one of those astral gateways, eh?'

They went back out to the parapet and were a little surprised to find the jinni waiting, standing stolidly in the sea doing his best to ignore the gulls flying around his head.

'The abbot has gone, I take it,' he said. 'I hope he appreciated the effort we went to on his behalf.'

'He did indeed,' said Altor. 'But why are you still here? I thought you'd be in a hurry to leave now the three wishes are used up.'

The jinni sucked at his moustache pensively. 'I was about to leave when it struck me that perhaps I still owe you half a wish, as I cannot deny I look some satisfaction in whipping those Tammuz priests. Thus I have decided to take you on to Hakbad as originally agreed – but mark my words, this is the last service I'll perform for you.'

'We can ask no more,' said Caelestis cheerfully. 'On, then – to Hakbad!'

The jinni scooped them in his hands and once more began the journey east. Though he took to the air and sped through the clouds, the dusk overtook them and by the time they were descending towards Hakbad it was against the velvet backdrop of night.

The full moon had risen, and in its light they saw great palaces and domed temples spread out below them. Unlike the crowded cities of the north, with their buildings crammed one upon the other between narrow streets,

Hakbad sprawled far and wide. Between the rooftops and the firelit windows lay long tracts of orchard, empty necropolis and dusty scrubland.

'See how Hakbad sits at the confluence of several rivers,' remarked the jinni, quite as if he were conducting a tour. 'In the early days there were numerous smaller settlements on this spot but, as they grew and merged, the City of Stars took shape.'

Caelestis saw the look in the jinni's eyes as he studied the streets beneath them. 'Do you know it well?'

'There was a time, now more than seventy decades past, when I was accustomed to take the form of a dog or merchant in order to stroll these very avenues.' As he descended to the ground they saw that the jinni was shrinking, and by the time he had set them down he was no taller than the palm tree that stood behind him.

'Your magic is versatile,' said Caelestis. 'You wouldn't care to exert yourself to find out where the blade of the Sword of Life is located, I suppose? I could offer you . . . well, this magic ring, for example.'

The jinni gave a laugh that became a bark as he shrank into the shape of a large black hound with glowing coals for eyes. As he ran off across the park, he called back: 'I said I'd do no more service for you or any mortal, but I will give you this last advice. Now you both have tasted death and lived again. The next time your souls travel to the afterlife it will be for a far longer stay – so beware, and farewell.'

They soon lost sight of him among the trees and Caelestis turned to Altor. 'Was that useful advice? It sounded ominous to me.'

'And cryptic, since I've never died.'

'Nor I.'

Altor considered resuming their argument but decided to drop it. He pointed to a gravel path that led out of the park. 'Susurrien said he'd wait for us – where?'

'At the House of the Desert Breeze. We

need to find someone who can tell us the way.'

They followed the path to a wide, tree-lined avenue bathed in moonlight. No one was about. The buildings in this part of the city showed no light at the windows. They loomed against the stars like shadowy mausoleums, seemingly abandoned.

Caelestis suddenly bent down and started to search for something in the gravel of the path.

'What are you up to?' said Altor.

Caelestis pocketed a couple of pebbles. 'Just an idea I had. I'll tell you about it later. Ah, here's someone . . .'

Down the avenue towards them came an old dervish carrying a heavy pack. Altor raised his hand to hail him. 'It's late to be out on the streets, good sir,' he said.

'Late – or early,' replied the dervish.

Seeing the puzzled look on Altor's face and realising that a discussion of philosophy might ensue, Caelestis stepped in. 'Do you know the way to the House of the Desert Breeze?'

'It is close by. Follow this avenue to the end, then look to your left. You will know the place you seek as its tower will be framed within the constellation of Arachnae the Spider.'

They soon identified the House of the Desert Breeze from the dervish's description. It was a low building faced in grey-green marble, enclosing a pair of courtyards. From a central structure between the courtyards rose the tower the dervish had mentioned: a thin spire covered with intricate carvings and surmounted by an iron-clad turret. The constellation known in Ta'ashim astronomy as the Spider seemed indeed to halo the tower. And something else as well – a milky opalescent bauble that hung low and louring among the stars . . .

'White Light,' said Caelestis. 'Can the other Magi be far behind?'

Altor squared his shoulders. 'Let's deal with

Susurrien first. Then we can worry about the Magi.'

They were kept waiting for several minutes in the stairwell of the tower, then a servant came with a lantern to escort them up. Susurrien's chambers were at the top, beyond a red-lacquered door deeply carved with leering demon-faces.

The room had a cloying air of musky incense. Dozens of thick candles stood on tall bronze stands, casting an uneven mix of light and shadow around the room. A mural along the opposite wall showed the pre-Ta'ashim gods of the region in scenes of sybaritic abandon. They looked almost alive in the flickering glow.

A curtain was flung aside and Susurrien swept into the room. He was dressed in a beige gown and white satin overrobe bordered with tassels of gold and sea-green. A pearl the size of a duck's egg glinted in the centre of his turban.

He smiled languidly. 'I expected you sooner. You have the Hatuli's eyes?'

Caelestis shrugged and reached into the folds of his toga, but Altor remained defiant. 'What assurance have we that you won't betray us?'

'Assurance?' Sussurien spread his hands. 'What assurance can I give? We are allies. I have the Hatuli, you have its eyes. Only by co-operating can we achieve what we desire. Our interests do not conflict. I have no use for the Sword of Life, any more than you have for the Sword of Death. Our goals are diametric, and there is surely no better guarantee against treachery than that.'

'There's one that is better.' Altor patted his sword. 'Remember that.'

Caelestis held out the emeralds. They reflected bright-green slashes of light across Susurrien's face as he stooped to examine them.

'Excellent, excellent,' he breathed. 'They are still redolent of Saknathur's sorcery even after so long.'

He fetched the Hatuli from a cabinet and

placed the emeralds in its empty eye-sockets before setting it down in the middle of a small table. Next he produced a brush and painted a gold spiral around it. Lastly he arranged twelve engraved onyx counters in a pattern at the edge of the spiral and intoned a brief spell.

Altor was watching Susurrien like a hawk, but Caelestis had his eyes on the Hatuli. He blinked. At the moment Susurrien completed his spell, he could have sworn he'd seen the grotesque little thing stand to attention.

Susurrien looked around, smiling broadly. 'The Hatuli is activated. It will take a few minutes to recharge its energy from the cosmic flux before it is able to move. Then it will find the Sword of Death for me.'

'Interesting,' said Caelestis. He stepped across to take a closer look, but caught his foot on the rug. Stumbling, he barged into the table and several of the onyx counters fell to the floor.

'Clumsy dolt!' snapped Susurrien, glowering at Caelestis as he recovered the counters.

'My apologies.' Seeing that the Hatuli had been knocked over, Caelestis set it back on its feet.

As suddenly as it had flared up, Susurrien's irritation vanished. Or was it only that his mask, having briefly slipped, was back in place? He turned and pointed to the mural. 'See this? It was found in a temple buried under volcanic ash. It predates the Ta'ashim faith, as you can see. Half a millennium ago, many of the people living in what is now Outremer and western Zhenir worshipped the gods depicted here.'

Altor glared at the mural. 'Did people really worship such vile and unclean monsters? I think they only feared them.'

Susurrien was delighted by Altor's reaction. 'You Coradians are so squeamish! But you are right, these deities were not loved. They were the devils of the old myths. When I said they were worshipped – well, in a way do you not worship the Devil of your own faith? His power is real because you believe in it. It is the strength of the myth that counts.'

'Preposterous. When can we depart? Is the Hatuli ready yet?'

'And so impatient. Look here: this serpentine creature with the three human heads. It is Azidahaka, the demon of destruction.' He pointed to another picture that showed a wizened man with the roots of a tree growing out of the top of his head. 'This is the Yazir, demon of deception and trickery. And here – here is Nasu, my favourite. She is the demoness of decay, depicted here as a bloated corpse with the head of a fly. If a man died from eating rotten food, the chances are that Nasu would be at the bottom of it.'

'Susurrien,' said Altor, 'your mural is distasteful and the "gods" shown in it are rank fiends. You yourself are sinister, if not openly depraved. So, if the Hatuli is now ready, let's take it and find the swords. Then we can bring this odious alliance to an end.'

Susurrien paused with his fingers on the

mural, then turned slowly to regard Altor. There was still an unruffled smile on his lips, but his eyes flashed with menace. 'I had not realised you held me in such contempt.'

Altor met his gaze squarely. 'You have been exiled from every country in which you have lived. That rather speaks for itself.'

Caelestis tried to defuse things. 'Why quarrel? We are poles apart – our goals diametrical, as you just said.'

Susurrien nodded. 'In fact you are right. I have no argument with the two of you, beyond the dislike I have for all your race and my scornful abhorrence of all self-righteous prigs. My motive is not malice, then, but curiosity.'

'Your motive for what?' growled Altor.

Susurrien gestured again at the mural. 'I have certain theories I wanted to test – theories about the nature of myth and reality. I believe that just as lenses can be used to form images of distant objects, so it should be possible to use focusing spells to create images of mythical beings. An image projected from the myth plane onto our own, so to speak. Do you find these concepts difficult to understand? Ah, you Coradians are so simple-minded. Allow me to demonstrate.'

He touched the pearl on his forehead and uttered something in a sibilant foreign tongue. Immediately the air became stifling, laden with menace like the oppressive atmosphere before a storm. The candles guttered low, threatening to plunge the room into darkness. As they flared up again, Altor and Caelestis sensed that something was wrong, but it took them a few seconds to grasp what it was.

Something stirred in the furthest corners of the room. Three huge shadows reared up.

It was then that they realised what had changed. The three demons were no longer in the mural.

Susurrien's magic had brought them to life.

THIRTEEN

The Sword of Life

Altor's sword sang as it left its scabbard. Cleansing light flashed from the blade. In the sickly yellow glow of he candles it was like a thread of pure uicksilver.

A heavy shape wove forward, and Altor saw hree narrow heads sprouting atop a long body f glistening black scales. The demon that usurrien had called Azidahaka. As it reared p, three human mouths opened with a hiss. he tongues were thin slivers that dripped vith poison, the teeth needle-shaped fangs.

Ignoring the hypnotic stare of those six ejewelled yellow eyes, Altor thrust his sword at the point where the necks joined the body. It struck the hard scales—

And broke in two.

Altor stood aghast with the stump of the blade in his hand. The gift of an elf sorceress, his sword had belonged to a legendary hero. He had grown to rely on its magic power. Certainly he had never imagined that anything on earth had the power to break it.

'Watch out!'

Caelestis grabbed Altor and pulled him out of the way just as the three demonic heads shot forward. There was an angry hiss as Azidahaka's jaws snapped shut on thin air. Poison splashed in a fine spray of droplets. One drop struck the back of Altor's hand and he gave a cry as it burnt his skin.

The pain helped him recover from the shock of seeing the sword shatter. Throwing the broken haft at the demon, he whirled to face Caelestis.

'Run?' said Caelestis, before Altor had even opened his mouth.

Altor nodded, and the two smashed through the red-lacquered door and flung themselves down the long staircase. From the room above issued a cacophony of shrieks and howls that echoed to horrible effect down the interior of the tower. It was a sound that had not been heard on earth since ancient times. The sound of immortals hunting human prey.

Halfway down they heard a jeering laughter and paused to look back. Three vast dark shapes formed baleful shadows on the stonework, slowly descending. On the landing above stood Susurrien, fingertips resting lightly on the iron frame of the balustrade as if he were gazing merely at a scene of casual interest.

'There can be no escape. My creatures are tireless. Wherever you flee they will pursue. When your legs are like water and your breath comes in fiery gasps, they will come relentlessly on. And at last they will seize you, ripping your frail flesh . . .'

They did not wait to hear more. Dashing

to the bottom of the stairs, they emerged into the courtyard. A tableau of soft blues and violets surrounded them, the palette of pre-dawn twilight. It was strange to look with pounding hearts on such a tranquil sight.

'Have you a plan?' gasped Altor.

'Sure,' said Caelestis sarcastically. 'We find three nice gods and get them to beat up Susurrien's lot.'

'Very helpful.'

'They broke your magic sword, for Heaven's sake! There's no plan that's going to work.' Caelestis started towards a narrow passage at the back of the courtyard. 'Come on, they're too big to fit through here.'

As they reached the passage there was a rush of musty air. A screech of inhuman bloodlust split the stillness of the night. Altor felt something snatch at him. Talons caught the back of his jacket but the fabric ripped. He ran on without looking back.

The passage opened into a street. Directly

opposite was a building with heavy locked doors and no windows.

Caelestis turned his gaze up to the symbol above the building's door. It was an embalming house. 'What irony,' he said bitterly.

Altor glanced back along the narrow passage to the courtyard. He had a glimpse of three hunched, hulking shapes that stared sullenly at him in the gloom. Then a gust of wind blew dust in his eyes, and when he looked again they were gone.

Caelestis was hammering at the door of the embalming house and cursing bitterly. Altor ran over, grabbed him by the arm and pulled him off along the street.

Another gust of hot wind blew down the street from behind them. They looked back as they ran. The three demon-things were there, looming against the paling sky.

'Do you think sunrise might banish them?' said Caelestis.

'Faint hope,' said Altor. 'Susurrien wouldn't overlook anything so obvious.'

A howl drew their attention to a nearby side-street. They looked in time to see a black dog lope off along it.

Without thinking they dived into the side-street. The three demon-gods came shambling, slithering, gibbering in pursuit.

The walls were six metres high on either side. Caelestis, who had once boasted he could scale a wall of polished glass, saw no handholds – and in any case there was no time to stop and look.

Behind, Altor again felt the hot, rank breath on his neck. He ran on, but now he knew that what Susurrien had said was true. The creatures would never give up. They would never tire. There was no escape.

Caelestis nearly tripped over the dog. The stupid creature had stopped to gawp at them.

Then he noticed the eyes, like hot coals . . .

There was a door in the wall of the alley. Leaves of silver filigree entwined the lock.

Hardly daring to hope, he pulled the key

that Fatima had given him from his robes. It, too, had large leaves engraved on it.

'Altor!' shouted Caelestis. He fumbled for the lock.

The demons were upon them, their stench a suffocating odour of evil. They reared up – three open maws slavering poison, old hands like gnarled roots, a buzzing many-eyed thing with the body of a swollen dead woman.

The door opened. Caelestis and Altor felt the dog speed between their feet as they flung themselves through. Sobbing in panic, Caelestis slammed the door. A heavy clout nearly knocked it open again. He jammed he key in the lock and turned it. With relief he heard the bolt click home.

On the other side, three ghastly voices were raised in a scream of frustrated fury. It rang out across the silent city, and as it faded Altor and Caelestis heard the grunts and resentful nuffling as the demons withdrew.

They slumped against the door. Apparently here they were safe. But for how long?

Catching their breath, they saw they were in a walled garden. The scent of jasmine filled their nostrils, as thick as the purple shadows of morning twilight. The grass under their feet was lush and damp with dew.

The dog bounded off across the lawn towards a pavilion where a woman sat sipping from a silver chalice.

It was Fatima, the sorceress they had met in Crescentium. She was instantly recognisable, even though she had worn a veil when they had rescued her from the Thulanders. Caelestis straightened himself and bowed.

Altor too. 'God bless you, lady,' he said. 'Your garden is a refuge from perils I think you would not believe.'

'I think I might.' Her voice was barely more than a murmur. 'Come and sit, and tell me what has befallen you since last we met.'

They joined her in the pavilion, but Caelestis could not restrain a worried glance at the high wall that ran around the garden. The demons could still be heard in the alleyway outside, scraping and tapping as they looked for a way in.

'You are sure that all doors to the garden are locked, Lady Fatima? Because—'

She smiled and offered them sweetmeats on a silver dish. 'All ways are locked, I assure you, and it is not often that I entrust others with the keys.'

She stroked the black dog that now lay at her feet. Altor looked at it and wondered. 'Is that . . . ?' He broke off, not quite sure how to phrase the question.

'Is that dog a jinni?' said Caelestis.

Fatima cocked an eyebrow. 'A jinni?' She laughed. 'Why ever should you think that?'

'It's just that we were brought to Hakbad by a jinni who – Oh, well, it's of no great importance.' He peered intently at the dog. 'He said he'd do no more favours for us, so I suppose it can't be.'

Now that they were out of danger, Altor had time to mull over the events of the last few minutes. 'We've failed,' he said. 'Even if we can somehow lose Susurrien's demons, he has the Hatuli. Without it we can't find the Sword of Life.'

'The Hatuli,' said Caelestis. 'Oh, yes.'

Out of his toga he drew a little wooden manikin with green gemstones for eyes.

Altor's jaw fell open. 'How . . . ?'

'Remember when we were on the island? I whittled a copy from a bit of driftwood, and I used some chips of green marble from the gravel path in the park for the eyes. Susurrien was too busy berating my clumsiness to notice the switch.'

'What a scheming knave you are!' said Altor cheerfully.

'Ah, the Hatuli,' said Fatima, picking it up. 'This was one of Saknathur's toys. And you want it to find the Sword of Life for you? It must be instructed in Ancient Kaikuhuran. *Ma'inir thiren qalash ne* – there, it's done.' She set the manikin down and it ran off across the lawn towards a gate half hidden by rosebushes.

Altor and Caelestis rose to follow it, pausing on the steps of the pavilion to look back at Fatima. 'Will we meet again?' asked Altor.

She nodded. 'Now, hurry. The Hatuli will take you to the blade. And remember that a weapon is only as strong as the courage with which it is wielded.'

They said farewell and let themselves out through the gate. It led to a small cobbled plaza with a well in the middle. On impulse, Caelestis looked back. There was no sign of the gate they had just come through, and he realised now that he had left the silver key on the table in Fatima's pavilion.

'Come on,' called Altor. He had followed the Hatuli to the edge of the well, where it was now waiting for them.

They peered down. The well was as dark as a grave. 'At least it seems dry,' said Caelestis.

Tucking the Hatuli in his belt, he started to climb down, calling out the location of handholds in the brickwork to Altor. At the bottom, the Hatuli came to life again.

It squirmed out of his belt and scurried to the back of the chamber in which they stood.

Altor lowered himself the last metre or so and waited while his eyes adjusted to the gloom. A little of the grey morning twilight penetrated into the depths, and they could see a jewelled door. Stalactites hung around it like tears.

'It can't have been opened for centuries . . .' said Caelestis in awe. He went forward and put his shoulder to the door. 'Help me, Altor.'

For several long minutes they bent in silence, straining all their muscles as they pushed against it. Gradually old limestone seals cracked, the accumulated dust and grit of many years was forced back, hinges fused solid with verdigris gave way. There was a sigh of inrushing air as the door opened a few centimetres.

From inside came a slow swirl of light, swimming with patterns of shade and brightness, just as sunlight, reflected from a river, writhes under the arch of a bridge.

The door swung open. The hall beyond was

half of white marble, half of black. To right and left, at either end, were vaulted alcoves in which stood blocks of grey stone.

On the left-hand block rested a sword-blade of jet-black metal that radiated flickers of shadow. To the right was a blade of so pure and intense a whiteness that it was almost painful to look upon.

Altor strode over to it, the hilt already in his hand. The pommel stone flared with rainbow colours in the white glare. Excitedly he fitted the blade in position and there was a sound like steel on an anvil as it locked in place.

Altor turned it in his hand, dazzled by the light. He tested the feel of it, swinging it around his head. It sliced through the air like an eagle's wing, sending pulses of light streaking from its aura to illuminate the dark corners of the room.

Altor raised it above his head and gave a great shout of joy. *'At last!'*

He had kept the promise made all that time ago in a forest glade in Krarth. After so long, so many hardships and dangers, the Sword of Life was whole again.

Caelestis could not keep his eyes from straying to the other blade. Darkness pulsated around it, like a rip in space that looked out onto the void.

'What about that one?'

'That's not for us,' Altor said, after a moment's thought. 'This is all we need to fight the Magi.'

They climbed back up the well-shaft full of optimism. Now that they had found and restored the Sword of Life, neither could quite believe it. Their quest fulfilled, they had the power now to keep the Five Magi from ever returning to earth. The grey sky above looked glorious.

Susurrien was waiting for them at the top of the well. With him were the three demons he had summoned.

FOURTEEN

The Pale Unsatisfied Ones

When Altor and Caelestis had entered the well it was still night. Now dawn was but a few minutes off. Under a silver sky, the buildings that before had seemed only indistinct shadows had taken on substance and the first hints of colour. A skyline of minarets and domes shimmered in the twilight. Now, with the cityscape revealed by approaching day, they noticed for the first time that they were close to the seafront. The bay stretched away glittering before them, a polished mirror under the dark frame of retreating night.

'Darkness on the one hand, dawn on the other. And here we stand in the thick of destiny,' said Susurrien.

Beside him the three resurrected gods stood outlined against the eastern sky, silent sentinels waiting to be appeased with human blood. The harsh light of the Sword of Life showed every monstrous detail: the tuberous scaly skin of the serpent, the alien visage and burst grey flesh of the disease-demon, the dark depravity in the Yazir's root-sunken eyes. Even Altor and Caelestis, who had experienced many horrors on their quest, felt the icy breath of fear.

It was Caelestis who noticed the silence. 'Where is everybody?' he said.

Altor looked around, ignoring the secret smile that formed on Susurrien's lips as he relished their perplexity.

Caelestis was right. At this hour, the city should be already coming to life. Where were the early traders on their way to market? Where were the priests shouting from the minarets, calling the faithful to dawn prayers?

Where were the birds, that should be singing in the trees?

It was with a shock that Altor heard Susurrien seem to read his mind. 'The bird of time has but a little way to fly, but I have clipped its wings. Under the wide sky, we alone share this moment – we three mortals, and these three gods of olden times, are all that stir from one rim of the world to the other.'

'You've frozen time,' said Altor, making it sound like a sin.

'Nobody's magic is that powerful,' said Caelestis.

Susurrien nodded. 'Good, good. You're right, of course, though I'm surprised you didn't realise it sooner. After all, if my own magic were enough to create simulacra of ancient gods and halt time, then I'd hardly have needed the Hatuli to locate a magic sword for me.'

Altor frowned. 'Then how . . . ?'

Caelestis understood. Rubbing his ring, he called out the Faltyn that lived within it. 'Here is something that belonged to Saknathur the wizard,' he said, holding up the Hatuli. 'Bring me the pearl from Susurrien's turban and you can have it.'

The Faltyn took a floating step towards Susurrien, only to hesitate like smoke caught in a back-draught. 'That jewel is White Light's gift. Not for all Saknathur's treasures will I aid you against the Magi, mortal.'

The Faltyn was staring past them into the western sky. Caelestis and Altor turned, following its gaze, and saw a sight that struck dread in their hearts. A sight that awakened in both of them memory of terrible dreams.

Against the curtain of night, five vast spectral shapes were visible, sparkling with dim colours like the northern aurora. A lord of green, another of gold, of blue and white and crimson. Five stern faces, sketched in ghost-light amid the fleeting stars, looked down at them with cold hatred.

Susurrien laughed as the Faltyn gave a whimper and curled back into its ring. 'You see now? The Magi gave me much power, but even they could not find the Sword of Life because it was hidden from them. That's all I needed you for.'

'So you intended to betray us right from the start?'

Altor took a pace towards him. The three demon-gods growled and heaved themselves forward. Altor stopped.

'Betrayal's such an ugly word,' said Susurrien. 'Also it implies personal animosity. I care not a whit about the two of you. To me you are just part of the common herd of humanity; you do not matter. But the Magi demanded your deaths as the price for the power they gave me, so you must see how it is . . .'

Caelestis shook his head. 'I see you're not your own master at all. You're just a puppet of the Five Magi.'

Susurrien clapped his hands in delight. 'You resort to name-calling now, Caelestis? You must be desperate. Well, I'll prolong this no further.'

He gave a signal to the demon-gods. Like three huge boulders, they swayed forward and began to close in on Altor.

'One question!' yelled Caelestis, mind whirring. 'Why have you stopped time?'

'According to prophecy, the Magi could return to earth neither until the sword was made whole, nor after it was. I've prolonged the instant that you found it, so that once you are slain they can descend and live again.'

'And you'll be the first one they dispose of!'

Susurrien winced. 'I'd heard reports you had a persuasive tongue, Caelestis. I must say you disappoint me.'

He half turned away, as if too fastidious to watch while his demons tore them limb from limb, and stood gazing out towards the bay where the five celestial lords glimmered in the western sky.

Caelestis had no weapon – he had lost his

dagger with his boots in the fireball at the temple of Tammuz. But he went to stand beside his friend as the three demons shuffled around to encircle them.

'Do you think there's any chance of defeating them now that we have the Sword of Life?'

Altor's eyes were fixed warily on the demon-gods. The thing with the fly's head made a probing feint towards him. He stabbed at it with the shining sword's tip. There was a hiss, a smell like charred hair, and the demon-god drew back its arm with a horrible buzzing cry that made Altor's skin crawl.

'Not much,' he said grimly. 'Even if I could kill one with a single blow, the other two would get us before I had time for another strike.'

'This is it, then.' Caelestis scowled at the sword, which looked like a shaft of pure energy in the grey twilight. 'That turned out to be a bit of a disappointment, didn't it?'

Altor's eyes flicked for a split second to

the sword. It was an almost fatal mistake. Seeing his concentration broken, the serpent-creature Azidahaka lashed out. Altor twisted aside without thinking and two of the heads missed, but the third clamped its jaws tight on his neck. Altor gasped as he felt stinging poison spurt into his veins.

Crack! The head released its grip and fell back, mouth gaping, eyes unfocused. Caelestis drew back his arm and gave Azidahaka another clout across the bridge of the nose with the manikin. This time the wood splintered and the Hatuli's legs went flying.

Azidahaka hissed and reared back, knocking Caelestis off his feet with an angry swish of its tail. It moved in for the kill. Caelestis struggled to stand, but one foot was caught under the demon-god's heavy coils. He looked up to see three narrow bald heads raised over him. Thin dark blood ran from one where the blow with the Hatuli had split its skin. Caelestis lay helpless. The worst thing, he thought, was that the creature showed no emotion. It was not hate that shone from its eyes, but only a cold, implacable viciousness.

The heads began to descend. Venom spattered like burning black rain. Caelestis braced himself for the fatal bite.

Out of nowhere Altor lunged forward. The Sword of Life blazed in his hand. Though he was staggering because of the poison in his bloodstream, his aim was true. Magic steel whispered through unhuman flesh, and one of the terrible heads fell to the ground.

It lay twitching, jaws pumping venom, while the demon-god thrashed and the remaining two heads screamed their fury to the heavens.

Altor's strength deserted him. He sat down heavily beside Caelestis. His hand opened and the sword lay across his limp palm. 'No use . . .' he gasped. 'It's not enough, Cael.'

Susurrien stood with his arms folded. Without turning to look at them, he gave an impatient sigh and said: 'Kill them now, so that I may enjoy the dawn.'

The other two demon-gods had hesitated

at seeing one of Azidahaka's heads sliced off. Now they pressed in towards the two heroes.

'We can't let it end like this,' said Caelestis. 'We have to fight.'

'Fight?' Altor swayed, bracing one arm against the ground to keep from falling flat. 'I can't even stand.'

'Not fight like that.' Caelestis shook his head vehemently, almost blinded by the sudden inspiration that flooded him. 'We've got it wrong, Altor – thinking of it as just a sword. It's a thing as old as Time itself. The mystery isn't how to wield it against three foes, it's how the power inside it can be contained at all!'

Altor looked at him through eyes half shut with pain.

Caelestis closed his hand over his friend's, so they both gripped the gleaming weapon's hilt. 'Have faith, Altor,' he said. 'This is the Sword of Life.'

In the stillness and silence of a frozen dawn, the demon-gods reached for them.

And then it came.

The first sign was a distant note, vibrating at the edge of hearing. Altor and Caelestis felt it through their fingertips even before they heard it. At the same time, the light from the sword-blade intensified.

The demon-gods faltered, the claws of the first just centimetres from Caelestis' face.

The note dropped from a high-pitched whine to a fierce irresistible shrieking. The demon-gods swayed as if in pain. The note continued to drop, becoming a low rumble that thrummed through the ground. It fell almost below the range of hearing.

And then, like a dam bursting, it swelled a thousandfold, seeming to speak with a voice of holy wrath. It was like the first sound in all Creation, a sound that could shake the world asunder – and with it came a blistering white light to match all the dawns there had ever been.

Squinting into the glare, the two heroes could just make out the flailing shapes of the demon-gods. They looked as if they were on fire, their essence evaporating in the flux of energy from the sword.

Susurrien stepped forward. 'I will kill you myself.' The words were almost drowned in the remorseless boom from the sword.

At his belt hung a scimitar. It was half out of its scabbard when he blundered into one of the demons. In its panic it turned, its arms thrown high to strike. Altor and Caelestis heard a short cry before Susurrien fell. They did not see him die – the blaze of white was too intense. All they could make out were three ragged shapes that fell on a cowering scrap of shadow and, in their blind fury, tore it apart.

The glare lessened, the noise began to subside. Altor and Caelestis were left with a ringing in their ears – and something else besides. The call to morning prayers, ringing across the rooftops of Hakbad.

A flock of birds took flight against the eastern sky, where a trace of gold now spilled up. They felt a breath of wind stir against their faces.

'Altor, it's the sunrise! Susurrien's spell—'

'—died with him.' Altor pointed to a bloody mess of ripped clothes and pulped flesh lying beside the well. The three demon-gods had vanished.

Caelestis got up and put out a hand to help his friend. Altor rose to his feet, a little surprised to still be alive. The wound on his shoulder was painful, but the poison had been burned out of his system.

They exchanged a look that said much: bliss to be alive; relief at victory; weariness and yet resolve; thankfulness for true friendship.

Together they remembered the Magi.

On the backdrop of the western sky, clothed in the last shreds of night, the five ghostly giants stood watching. A wave of implacable hatred radiated down from them, though their faces might have been as distant and unmoving as the farthest nebulae.

Altor lifted the sword. 'You've seen the

Sword of Life, you know now what it can do. Hide in the heavens. Or come down to earth and be destroyed!'

The blade, catching the rays of the rising sun, flared anew with light.

For the first time, the Magi showed emotion. Their eyes narrowed in discomfort or distaste. They turned, ponderous as vast clouds, towards the west – and then were swept away by daybreak. All that remained to be seen were the five comets, and soon those, too, were lost against the lightening sky.

'I hope we've seen the last of them,' said Caelestis.

He turned away to see a crowd gathering. With the flow of time restored, people were coming from their houses to investigate. Someone pointed to Susurrien's remains.

Altor and Caelestis hurried away. 'We don't need any more trouble like my experiences in Crescentium,' said Caelestis.

Altor nodded. 'Absolutely. All I want is to find an inn where I can get this wound bandaged, wolf down a hearty breakfast, and then sleep for a week.'

'And I can get some decent clothes instead of this makeshift toga.'

'Except that we're penniless as usual.'

'*Penniless*, certainly,' said Caelestis, with a smile. He reached into the folds of his robe and drew out a gold medallion. 'This would be a worth a few hundred florins, though.'

Altor stopped and looked at him accusingly. 'Where did you get that, Caelestis?'

'In Saknathur's tower, while you were talking to the abbot. We originally stopped there to search for trinkets, you'll recall.'

Altor laughed. 'Ah, well! Why shouldn't heroes do well while doing good? Lead on, then, my friend – let's find the finest inn in Hakbad!'

Epilogue

In the middle of the street stood a grove of palm trees around an ornamental pool, like an island in a river of packed dirt. Caelestis looked up as he passed, thinking to see a slender figure standing under the trees, but no one was there.

A figure in warlock's robes watched them go. Then, hidden by the cloak of his invisibility spell, he wove his way through the gathering crowds. He spared Susurrien's body hardly a glance. Another spell sparked from his fingertips, and when he stepped over the edge of the well it was to drift lightly down into the cool darkness.

Epilogue

The door to the secret chamber stood open. 'How slovenly of them,' said the warlock to himself. 'Anyone might have wandered in and found it.'

He entered a chamber that was bathed now only in rippling darkness – no longer like the surface of a river, but its dim impenetrable depths.

In reaching for the black blade, he paused. The waves of darkness emanating from it slid like gossamer across the sharp contours of his face. Glittering tawny eyes, almond in shape, drank their fill of it.

As he took hold of the Sword of Death he gave a moan of pleasure, although the sharp edge cut his hand. He licked away the drops of blood as he studied his prize. It throbbed, full of sorcery, avid for him to use it.

'And use you I shall,' he said, answering his own thoughts. 'I have a fine and private purpose in mind, a purpose that shall turn the recent victory of my two dear foes to dust.

They shall suffer a thousand terrors before they die. So I swear, Lord Utayama-no-Sugensiki Aiken – called, in this heathen land, Icon the Ungodly.'